Hierarchy of

(Relic Hunters #10)

By
David Leadbeater

Copyright © David Leadbeater 2023
ISBN: 9798854055475

All rights reserved.
No part of this publication may be reproduced, distributed, or transmitted in any form or by any means, including photocopying, recording, or other electronic or mechanical methods, without the prior written permission of the publisher/author except in the case of brief quotations embodied in critical reviews and certain other non-commercial uses permitted by copyright law.

All characters in this book are fictitious, and any resemblance to actual persons living or dead is purely coincidental.

Classification: Thriller, adventure, action, mystery, suspense, archaeological, military, historical, assassination, terrorism, assassin, spy.

Other Books by David Leadbeater:

The Matt Drake Series

A constantly evolving, action-packed romp based in the escapist action-adventure genre:

The Bones of Odin (Matt Drake #1)
The Blood King Conspiracy (Matt Drake #2)
The Gates of Hell (Matt Drake 3)
The Tomb of the Gods (Matt Drake #4)
Brothers in Arms (Matt Drake #5)
The Swords of Babylon (Matt Drake #6)
Blood Vengeance (Matt Drake #7)
Last Man Standing (Matt Drake #8)
The Plagues of Pandora (Matt Drake #9)
The Lost Kingdom (Matt Drake #10)
The Ghost Ships of Arizona (Matt Drake #11)
The Last Bazaar (Matt Drake #12)
The Edge of Armageddon (Matt Drake #13)
The Treasures of Saint Germain (Matt Drake #14)
Inca Kings (Matt Drake #15)
The Four Corners of the Earth (Matt Drake #16)
The Seven Seals of Egypt (Matt Drake #17)
Weapons of the Gods (Matt Drake #18)
The Blood King Legacy (Matt Drake #19)
Devil's Island (Matt Drake #20)
The Fabergé Heist (Matt Drake #21)
Four Sacred Treasures (Matt Drake #22)
The Sea Rats (Matt Drake #23)
Blood King Takedown (Matt Drake #24)
Devil's Junction (Matt Drake #25)

Voodoo soldiers (Matt Drake #26)
The Carnival of Curiosities (Matt Drake #27)
Theatre of War (Matt Drake #28)
Shattered Spear (Matt Drake #29)
Ghost Squadron (Matt Drake #30)
A Cold Day in Hell (Matt Drake #31)
The Winged Dagger (Matt Drake #32)
Two Minutes to Midnight (Matt Drake #33)

The Alicia Myles Series

Aztec Gold (Alicia Myles #1)
Crusader's Gold (Alicia Myles #2)
Caribbean Gold (Alicia Myles #3)
Chasing Gold (Alicia Myles #4)
Galleon's Gold (Alicia Myles #5)
Hawaiian Gold (Alicia Myles #6)

The Torsten Dahl Thriller Series

Stand Your Ground (Dahl Thriller #1)

The Relic Hunters Series

The Relic Hunters (Relic Hunters #1)
The Atlantis Cipher (Relic Hunters #2)
The Amber Secret (Relic Hunters #3)
The Hostage Diamond (Relic Hunters #4)
The Rocks of Albion (Relic Hunters #5)
The Illuminati Sanctum (Relic Hunters #6)
The Illuminati Endgame (Relic Hunters #7)
The Atlantis Heist (Relic Hunters #8)
The City of a Thousand Ghosts (Relic Hunters #9)

The Joe Mason Series
The Vatican Secret (Joe Mason #1)
The Demon Code (Joe Mason #2)
The Midnight Conspiracy (Joe Mason #3)
The Babylon Plot (Joe Mason #4)

The Rogue Series
Rogue (Book One)

The Disavowed Series:
The Razor's Edge (Disavowed #1)
In Harm's Way (Disavowed #2)
Threat Level: Red (Disavowed #3)

The Chosen Few Series
Chosen (The Chosen Trilogy #1)
Guardians (The Chosen Trilogy #2)
Heroes (The Chosen Trilogy #3)

Short Stories
Walking with Ghosts (A short story)
A Whispering of Ghosts (A short story)

All genuine comments are very welcome at:

davidleadbeater2011@hotmail.co.uk

Twitter: @dleadbeater2011

Visit David's website for the latest news and information:
davidleadbeater.com

Hierarchy of Madness

CHAPTER ONE

It was one of those drab, dreary, grey New York mornings when all the colours seem to be leeched from the day, when the rising sun hasn't quite breached the horizon, when the greyness of early morning is everywhere: in the two and three-storey buildings to the left, in the high-rises beyond, in the pavement and in the asphalt that lined the road, in the rolling Hudson River to the right, the faces of fellow joggers, the curtained and draped windows that, at this time of the morning, didn't even twitch.

Cassidy Coleman loved it. Despite this being central New York, she felt alone. The world was fresh, made anew. She put her head down and she ran from the hotel along Riverside Drive, conscious that she was on her own in the world... apart from the odd other, wrapped-up jogger who panted past.

The city that never sleeps was at least drowsing, she thought. Even the roads, New York City's lifeblood, were peaceful, serene, running smooth and free before the build-up of traffic would come to choke the arteries later. Cassidy breathed deep, slowing for a while, conscious of her surroundings.

Cassidy used these quiet mornings to think. It was her getaway, that time before life really got going, intruding necessarily into her day. It only lasted an hour but, often, it was the best hour of the whole twenty-four.

She stopped at an intersection, tugged her hood from her head and let it lie across her shoulders. She was warming up, starting to sweat, her heartbeat rising. Only one car passed, its rubber tyres rumbling across the asphalt, its exhaust rumbling. Cassidy waited for the lights to change, jogging on the spot. Soon, she was off again, pounding the pavement, letting her thoughts run free.

Two weeks had passed since they returned from the Amazon and the city of a thousand ghosts. Since then, the governments had got involved in the discovery, complicating everything. Treasure wasn't treasure when it came to the manipulation and greed of governments. It was a commodity, something to be owned and profited from. Still, at least it was safe from secret cults and madmen.

She hoped.

They had come to New York at the request of the American government, found a place to stay, and then proceeded to go through what remained of their funds, paying for it. As a group, and as individuals, their net worth was dwindling rapidly. The government had come to them, taken down their statements regarding the Amazon adventure, and gone away. That had been a week ago. The team met nightly, trying to decide what to do next, wondering if any reward might be due to them for their discovery. Technically, there was. Realistically, Bodie and the others doubted they'd ever see it.

And that put them in quite the predicament.

Since they'd escaped the clutches of Pang and the CIA, the Relic Hunters had been mostly jobless. Yes, they'd foiled the Atlantis heist and done well in the Amazon, but none of that paid the bills, helped them stay afloat. Where exactly did they go from here?

Bodie's joke was that they should rob from rich, criminal folk, as he used to do in his youth. He'd enlist the services of good old Jack Pantera, his old boss, and steal from those who deserved it. The others had looked at him with wondering eyes even as they laughed, hoping he wasn't reverting to old ways.

He wasn't.

At least, Cassidy hoped not. Her old ways were not something she'd like to visit. She'd grown up hard and fast on the streets of Los Angeles, leaving home at the age of seventeen, never having been mistreated physically but never having been loved or wanted. She didn't see her parents again, fell in love with an older guy who later died, then fell in with a dangerous man but saw it in him and left before anything happened. She had been homeless for a while, fought as an underground street fighter and even got bit parts in a few Hollywood movies. When she was nineteen, Cassidy's boyfriend had taught her the meaning of love. She hadn't understood it. But he had held her, comforted her, and stayed with her and said *'this is love.'* Love was belonging, feeling *together*. It was letting go of ego and your own needs. She had never understood, not until then.

Cassidy had quit the underground street fighting game when she saw she was going to get killed. She had met Guy Bodie, fallen in with him and his gang, and never looked back. They had been together ever since and had both come up with the saying: *family is a sense of belonging*. Cassidy loved being part of a team, and wouldn't have it any other way.

But these New York mornings... they were different. Cassidy's persona was extrovert... she was a partygoer, a gregarious social butterfly. But every extrovert needed a few reclusive moments. They'd explode if they didn't get them, she imagined. Or at least, *she* would.

Cassidy was comfortable with who she was. She had reached her place in life in many ways, and was happy. Her worries centred around what would happen to the relic hunter team if they didn't find a form of monetary sustenance. They had contacts. Lucie had them through her historian background; Heidi through her ex-CIA credentials. Yasmine was ex-Interpol and Bratva and knew people from every walk of life. And Jemma? Well, Jemma was a cat burglar and tech extraordinaire, but she didn't have a lot of friends.

Cassidy smiled as she ran, as the greyness painted her face the colour of newspaper.

And then there was... Reilly.

The newcomer had stayed with them since the Amazon, at the request of the government at first. Reilly was an adventurer, a finely chiselled, fit, Levis wearing dude with life experience of the Bratva and years living on the edge as an explorer. He was a man who had escaped the attentions of criminals by going to the Amazon and working with more criminals, his sense of good and duty forcing him even then to report the worser ones. He was a good man, Cassidy sensed, just mixed up with bad life choices and a sense of being hunted.

Reilly fully expected the Bratva to come looking for him, to kill him for desertion. Cassidy thought he'd done enough by disappearing in the Amazon for years.

And to top it all, Reilly was Yasmine's ex-boyfriend. Nobody quite knew how that scenario was going to play out, but the two of them were being hyper mature about it so far.

Hierarchy of Madness

Cassidy continued on her way, air cushioned trainers coming down hard on the pavement, breath hissing through her teeth. The sweat was cold across her forehead, her limbs burning nicely. She ran, she processed, she kept an eye on her surroundings. With regret, she saw the sun just coming up, sneaking over the horizon to the east, barely seen through the cluster of buildings in that direction. As if to signify its birth, the morning seemed to get busier. Coffee shops opened. More cars clogged the intersections. Oblivious people walked in her path. She was suddenly glad she was on her backward loop, headed for the hotel, and resolved to set off even earlier the next morning.

The peaceful moments weren't long enough.

Cassidy kept going, seeing the wall in front of her and breaking through. Sweat dripped from her face. The rumble of a passing vehicle drew her attention. She saw a black van with some kind of fish logo on its sides, just grumbling past. She looked away, didn't make eye contact with the driver, didn't want to draw the attention. She wasn't ready for human contact just yet.

The day marched on, unstoppable. Cassidy saw the attention she attracted from passers-by, but ignored it. She was a striking redhead, six feet tall, and drew glances even with her hair tied back, her baggy running clothes on, and her face bright red. Cassidy never acted shy, never looked away from prying eyes. She was confident, brash, confrontational even. But there were moments when you just wanted to be a hermit.

Running brought that out in her. She loved the part of her life when, just for an hour, she could be a different person.

The buildings marched towards her hotel. She couldn't see it yet, but there was a small green area up ahead fronted by black iron railings. She liked to pause there just for a few moments, with the railings at her back, looking out over what small part of the Hudson she could see, peering into the distance. It was part of her morning ritual. After that she would run on to the hotel, pausing at the local coffee shop for black coffee and croissants that she couldn't really afford, before heading back up to her room, showering and then wondering what the rest of her day would bring.

She reached the railings, paused, grabbed hold of one of them, and panted. She wiped sweat from her face, turned around. Traffic sped by. Later, it would crawl like slow-moving sludge. The greyness all around was being leached now, replaced by the rising golds and reds of a fresh morning, and she loved seeing that too. Loved being a part of the fresh hour. Since arriving in New York and starting this ritual, Cassidy already knew it was one she wanted to partake in indefinitely. It called to her. Called to her like adventure and good times and friends.

Her eyes never stopped moving. She checked the green area, the park swings, the road, the pavements. She saw the slow-moving vehicles, the lingering walkers, the men and women with their dogs on leashes and some without. Cassidy was always alert; it was how she'd spent the last twenty years of her life.

The fish van went by again.

This time it was travelling fast. Cassidy got a glimpse of two men in the front, but didn't think much of it. They could be lost, turned around. It might even be a different van; she hadn't noted the original license plate.

She caught her breath. The coffee and croissants were beckoning. She took a last look around and then put her head down, prepared to set off on the last leg of her run.

The fish van pulled up to the kerb with a squeal of brakes.

Cassidy whirled around.

CHAPTER TWO

The black van shuddered as people moved about quickly inside the back. Someone threw the sliding door open. A man stepped from the front, leaving the driver alone. Men leapt out of the black, all clad in black and wearing face masks.

It left Cassidy in no doubt as to what was happening here.

She had no room. The pavement was narrow. The men climbed out of the van right into her face. She had a momentary advantage as they stepped down to the ground and did all she could to make use of it.

The first man who clambered out received a kick to the groin, folding him in half. The second got a punch to the face that sent him reeling. A third received a kick from her other foot, but they kept coming. Three became four, and then five, and more.

The man who'd exited the front of the vehicle came in from the side. He swung a haymaker at her face. Cassidy fell back, tight against the railings, and the fist brushed past her nose, just scraping by. She grabbed the man's arm, twisted it, and forced him to the ground.

By then, more men had jumped out of the side.

She saw she was facing eight men. Two were on the floor, another holding his face. She hit out again, making them wary of her, sending two more men staggering away. But there were too many. Cassidy was heavily outnumbered, even with her skills.

She looked calmly left and right, saw empty pavement both ways. The small green area was at her back, and she chose that way, noticing hedges and trees and a far gate. She was a runner. Cassidy would run for it.

She pivoted, ran along the railings with the men chasing her. A couple of cars passed, but the driver's views might have been blocked by the van still idling at the kerb. Cassidy swung a fist out blindly, struck someone in the face, maybe the eyes. It was a good strike. She reached the open gate and ran through.

The park was deserted. She pounded along a winding path with a slight incline. Hedges lay to left and right, barely waist high. She felt the men at her back, running hard. She risked a quick glance, saw all eight of them in pursuit and the van moving forward so that it was now parked opposite the entrance, its sliding doors still open.

There were no words spoken, no sounds other than panting and the pounding of feet. Cassidy jumped on a bench and then whirled. She kicked out from on high, catching a running man right across the face. He didn't utter a sound, just went down like a sack of spanners, hitting the grass hard. He didn't move after that. Cassidy didn't pause for a second, just leapt over the back of the bench before she could get swamped and ran a different way.

One down, seven to go.

She sprinted hard, staying about four steps ahead of her pursuers. She saw another bench, didn't think they'd fall for the same trick twice, but pretended to do it, anyway. Cassidy leapt on the bench. They slowed.

She didn't, running on and gaining a few more steps. She was sweating hard, panting, already tired from her run that morning and now being forced to race at top speed.

She wasn't going to escape. Cassidy instinctively knew it, though she could run and run and try to find a busier area. That was the goal. Maybe it had been a mistake to enter the park. Maybe she should have just run out into the road, flagged passing cars down. But the van had pulled up on the road; it had been highly visible. The men didn't seem to care that they were in the open. Of course, they were wearing face masks, and the van was probably stolen, or wearing stolen plates.

Cassidy ran downhill now as the path followed a straight line past a swing-set to the rear gate. That gate was wide open. Cassidy veered to the right, ran among the swings and lifted one, swung it viciously backwards. The swing connected with a man's running face, felling him again without a sound. That left six of them.

Could she take them in a full-on fist fight?

Cassidy was confident in her abilities, but success really lay in the skills of the men she faced. If they weren't very good, she might win. But if they were trained, hardened mercenaries, she didn't stand a chance. Not against six.

She glanced back, saw nothing in their masks, nothing to guess at what or who they were. Just a mass of racing bodies. She saw knives at their belts, no guns and no backpacks. Just short-bladed weapons.

Cassidy ran for the gate. She had another trick up her sleeve, but it didn't work. She span and kicked out, delivering a spinning kick with great power that just missed the man closest to her. Then she was inundated by attackers, barely able to stay ahead of the pack. She ran out of the gate and under a row of trees, shaded and dark and cool. The pavement curved ahead, veering to the right. She kept going, breathing heavily. In her pocket were her mobile phone and her room key. She wondered if she might make use of the phone, perhaps call Bodie and the others, to get some help.

What the hell was happening here?

Why did they want her? Cassidy knew she'd been targeted, singled out. Was it just a random snatching? She doubted it, not with this many men chasing her. A random attack would have been precisely that, carried out by one or maybe two men. This was a concerted effort to grab one woman – *her*.

She came out from the tree cover, found herself on another street. She didn't slow, just kept barrelling along. Adding to her consternation was the sight of the black van with the fish logo turning out of a side street up ahead and driving closer, ever closer, keeping track. The sliding doors were still open, the driver watching carefully.

Cassidy had few choices. There were a few people here and there, some waiting at bus stops, others sauntering along the opposite pavement. Could they see what was happening? Did they want to get involved? Would they call the cops? Maybe... not definitely. And how long would it take for the cops to answer the call?

Cassidy was running out of time.

She had minutes and ran into the road, but at first there were no cars. She ran down the centre line. When one car did approach, it wanted nothing to do with the situation, veering into the opposite carriageway to get away from the running men and women. Cassidy didn't blame the driver – what could one man do?

Hopefully, make a phone call, she thought.

But she was at the end of her tether. She was slowing, but maybe so were the men following her because they hadn't caught up. She needed to put up a fight whilst she still had the strength to do so.

Cassidy fumbled in her pocket, found her phone and tried to use the speed dial feature on the run. It was impossible at top speed; the screen jiggling around out of time to her fingers, the device actually slowing her down even more.

She glanced back once more. Six men were close, and now she saw the two she'd already felled, following more slowly some way behind. There would be no stopping them. Just then, a pursuer put on a sprint, caught Cassidy up. she waited and then lashed out with an elbow, striking the side of his face even as they both continued running. She thrust the phone back in her pocket, lashed out again. This time the guy blocked, but she followed the elbow strike with a backhand to the ribs that caught him off guard. He staggered, reached out to pull her down with him.

Cassidy put on a burst of speed that took her away from his grasp, but it was a costly burst of speed. It tapped the rest of her reserves, made her lungs scream, sent jelly flooding her legs. She had to slow down or she would fall down.

She whirled then, facing five running men. The first was easy. He wasn't ready for her sudden move. She moved aside and flung out a leg, tripping him. The guy flew past her, headlong, scraping the pavement. The second and third ran into her strikes, one an elbow, the other a fist, and stumbled to left and right. Two more running attackers slowed, their breath screeching from their mouths, their shoulders slumped.

As Cassidy waited, one of them flung himself at her.

There was no escaping the attack. He hit her in the chest, pushed her backwards so that she retreated at speed, with no idea what was behind her. The other men had recovered now and were closing in, too.

Now Cassidy stood her ground. This was it. There would be no more retreating, no more running. She punched left and right, catching the men across their faces and ducking their own blows. She kicked out, dancing from foot to foot, felling two but taking a heavy blow to the stomach. Cassidy staggered.

She folded.

The men were all over her, punching. The light of the day was blocked by the van that slid up to the kerb. She recognised the fish logo, the sliding door still wide open. She wasn't done yet, even though she felt overwhelmed. Cassidy squeezed a man's scrawny neck until he yanked himself away in agony. She kneed a man in the groin, head-butted another until blood flooded across his face and the shoulders of the man beside him. She hit out with everything she'd got, injuring all of them, making them retreat and regroup and come at her again. They were faceless, practically noiseless, just empty masks filling her field of vision. She felt horror; revulsion, but most of all, she just felt anger.

Cassidy was weakening, knew she was done if she stayed on the ground, letting them crawl around her. Punches landed intermittently, but on all sides. One to her left ribcage, another to her right thigh, then another to the side of her head. She couldn't pick out a single man, had to hit them all, and that caused her punches to be weaker, less focused. She got a quick glimpse of the pavement all around and saw it was deserted. Someone jogged by on the other side of the street, watching, a phone to his ear.

Maybe the cops would get here yet.

A blow landed on her forehead, another on her left temple. The scene swam by; she felt lethargic. Sat up, took a deep breath, hit out with fists and elbows. She got to her knees. There was a sudden weight that struck her back like a boulder, slamming her back down to the ground, and then blows rained in from all sides.

Cassidy groaned, weakened. Her limbs felt heavy, her focus blurred. The men grabbed her arms, her legs. They were eight strong once more. She had achieved nothing except to tire herself out. The open van door was to her left, the inside as dark and welcoming as an unfathomable cave. The men swung her one way and then the other, and then let go. She shot into the van, hit the metal floor, rolled.

She tried to stand up.

Her legs were jelly, her vision blurred. They jumped in and hit her again. They filled the entire back of the van, just men with fists and boots, all aimed at her.

She fell to her knees.

The men grabbed her phone from her pocket and threw it back out onto the pavement.

The last thing she saw was a plastic bag being hurled out of the open door. It hit the street and rolled and, through the open top, before the door slammed shut, she saw a ragged, severed head.

CHAPTER THREE

Guy Bodie woke feeling content and rested. Sunlight streamed in through the thin drapes that covered the hotel room's window, soaking him in warmth. He stretched. He yawned. For a moment, he felt wonderful, and there were no worries plaguing his already overworked mind.

Just for a moment.

Bodie sat up in bed. *Back to reality.* They couldn't stay here much longer. One outlet was to ask their CIA contact, Kenny Pang, for a job. But Bodie didn't want that. It had taken them years to get out from under the thumb of the CIA. No way was he getting re-involved.

Bodie rose and walked to the mirror. He was wearing only boxer shorts, his muscled body scarred with old wounds. Bodie had a strong build, was closely shaven on the head and the chin, and had always had ridiculously white teeth. He was a solitary man, finding it hard to socialise, but when he found the right people, he did all he could to nourish and hold on to them. A great friend and colleague was as rare as gold dust these days and Bodie believed he had found five of them. Cassidy and Jemma had been around for years, part of his family now. Yasmine and Lucie were relatively new, but had earned his respect and his admiration. Heidi... well, Heidi was different.

Heidi Moneymaker had helped pluck Bodie from the

Mexican prison where he might've died, and then put him to work for the CIA. Over the years, they had got closer and closer until now... well, their relationship was as close to the next level as it would ever get.

Did Bodie want the next level?

Did Heidi? That was the question. Bodie stared at himself in the mirror. Crap, it shouldn't be this hard. He should just go for it. Perhaps... today...

Another thought intruded. Thinking of being forthright reminded Bodie of the newcomer, Reilly. If Reilly didn't fancy Cassidy, then Bodie's first name wasn't Guy. The thing is, Bodie liked Reilly. He was an adventurer and, judging by their journey through the Amazon, a reliable, hard-working, intelligent individual. He was still with them, primarily because of the government debrief. Bodie liked Reilly and felt for the man. He was being hunted... maybe. And maybe the Bratva hadn't got wind of his time in the Amazon. It was going to be hard for Reilly in the future.

But Bodie wanted to help him. He wasn't sure how he felt about Reilly fancying Cassidy, but it really wasn't any of his business. The tricky bit came with Reilly being Yasmine's ex. Bodie sighed, not wanting to get too deep at this time of the morning.

He stood up, padded to the bathroom. He ran the shower and jumped in, treated himself to a long soak. It was when he was exiting the bathroom, towelling off, that his phone rang.

Bloody typical.

Naked, he scooped it up from the bed, noted the call was coming from Cassidy, and put it to his ear.

'Hello?'

'Who is this?' a male caller asked.

Bodie frowned. 'Guy,' he said warily. 'Who's this? Where's Cassidy?'

Hierarchy of Madness

'Sir, this is Detective Wright of the NYPD. I'm assuming you know the person who's registered to this phone?'

'Yeah, her name's Cassidy. What are you doing with it?' Bodie was at a loss.

'I need you to come down to Riverside Drive right now, sir. I need to talk to you.'

Bodie frowned. 'What's going on?'

There was a loud sigh from the other end of the line. In the background Bodie could hear voices and the sound of someone shouting, the noise of a far-away ambulance.

'We're calling because you are the first person registered on Cassidy's speed dial,' the cop said. 'Let me give you an address.'

'Wait,' Bodie said. 'Is Cassidy okay?'

There was no answer. The cop reeled off an address, something about West 80th and Riverside with a coffee shop nearby. Bodie felt a chill when he realised that wasn't far from the hotel.

'What's going on?' he asked again. Anxiety had robbed him of his vocabulary.

'I'll explain it all when you get down here. Hurry, please.'

Bodie listened to the end of the call, the silence and then a dial tone. He pressed the red button on the screen. He looked around, not seeing the hotel room, the walls, the blinds on the windows. His heart was hammering, his throat dry.

Cassidy?

Why would cops be using her phone? Why wasn't *she* calling? The answer was terrible no matter which way you looked at it.

Within minutes, he had gathered the team in the

17

lobby downstairs. Everyone looked erratic, unready, wary, scared. Jemma, always quiet, stood in a corner, her long dark hair done up in a severe bun, her face strained. Her arms were folded, and she looked like she wanted to be anywhere but here. Close to her stood Yasmine, her black hair hanging past her shoulders, her eyes locked on his. Worry was plastered across her face like a challenge. Lucie stood with her arms folded, a small figure. And then there was Heidi. The ex-CIA agent was biting her lip. Her frizzy hair hung around her face. Heidi was both driven and lonely, but today she just looked scared.

Bodie faced them, the same expression no doubt creasing his own face.

'We don't know what's happened,' he said. 'I suggest we find out as soon as we can.'

'They're cops,' Heidi reminded them all. 'They'll give away as little as possible whilst trying to get you to sing like a bird.'

'We have nothing to hide,' Jemma said.

For a change, Bodie thought, and then shrugged it away. It wasn't helping.

'Yeah, they're gonna be interested in our history,' Yasmine said.

It was true. The cops would liken their relic hunting past to... to what? Bodie knew they were just clutching at straws and wasting time. Still, it didn't hurt to go in prepared.

'Our history doesn't matter,' he said. 'It's up to date. We have no enemies floating around, and neither does Cassidy. We were being interviewed by the government until a few days ago, for God's sake. They picked up our hotel tab.'

'Shall we find out what's happened before we draw any conclusions?' Heidi said.

Bodie nodded.

'I have enemies,' Reilly said.

Bodie hesitated. Damn, he'd forgotten their new friend. Reilly was leaning nonchalantly inside a niche in the wall, fitting perfectly, his electric blue eyes lasered in on all of them. Bodie shook his head at the man.

'You don't have to come with us,' he said.

'But I want to. I care for Cassidy too. I may not be a part of the team, but I still want to help.'

Bodie nodded. 'I doubt the Bratva will come after you, mate.'

Reilly nodded. 'Maybe.' He didn't look convinced.

'Well, they certainly wouldn't come after Cassidy,' Yasmine said. 'No way is this the Bratva.'

Bodie looked to the lobby doors. 'Let's go find out what *this* is,' he said.

CHAPTER FOUR

The detective in charge approached Bodie as he stood on the other side of the crime scene tape.

'Come under,' he said. 'All of you.'

Bodie ducked and walked under the yellow tape, followed by the others. It was a surreal scene. A portion of the pavement had been taped off, the yellow tape anchored between tree trunks and the black railings that lined the pavement. There were splashes of something dark at random spots on the ground, spots that could only be dried blood. There was a bevy of looky-loos, two police cars and a van, a herd of crime scene investigators and one or two uniformed cops. The road itself was open, the crime scene contained to the pavement.

'Detective Wright,' the man who'd ushered them inside the tape said. He wore a long coat and had thick facial hair. His beady eyes poked from underneath wide brows, and even the backs of his hands were hairy. He held up a black plastic device.

'Are you Guy Bodie?'

Bodie nodded. 'What happened to Cassidy?' he asked.

'We're working on it,' Wright answered, indicating the crime scene. 'What is Cassidy to you?'

'A good friend. Who are all these people?' Bodie had just noticed four men and women standing next to the police van looking bored.

'Eye witnesses. Do you know anyone who might want to abduct Cassidy?'

Bodie stared, his mouth suddenly the texture of dried cement. His lips parted, but nothing came out. The words wouldn't come. Finally, it was Jemma who said: 'I don't know anyone who *could* abduct Cassidy.'

Wright zeroed in on her. 'What do you mean by that?'

Bodie finally found his voice. 'Cassidy's an ex-fighter. Well trained. She's stronger than all of us. It would take-'

'Eight men,' Wright said, consulting his notes. 'Or maybe men and women. The eye witness statements are poor at best. It was very early, and they wore masks.'

'Eight people abducted Cassidy?' Heidi sounded like she didn't believe it.

'Chased her down. Fought with her. Dragged her into a van.'

'Plates?' Heidi was reverting to being a cop herself.

'Found it abandoned. Burnt out. Four miles from here.'

'CCTV?' Heidi asked.

'Who the hell are you? My boss?' Wright stared at her suspiciously.

'I watch a lot of cop shows.'

Wright grunted. 'Well... the CCTV is active around here. Not so much where they dumped the van, which they probably knew. We do not know what vehicle they switched to.'

'What do you have from the local CCTV?' Bodie asked.

But now Wright was regarding them with interest, sensing something. He looked them over more carefully. 'Who are you guys?' he asked.

Bodie was tempted to say, *'We're the Guardians of the Galaxy,'* but prudence and fear for Cassidy restrained him. He said nothing.

Wright licked his lips. 'Look,' he said. 'There's no easy way to say this. Do you have a photo of Cassidy?'

Bodie narrowed his eyes. 'A photo? Yeah. But why say it like that?'

Wright sighed. 'The abductors left something at the crime scene. I need one of you to take a look so we can rule something out.'

Bodie said, 'You're being a bit vague here, mate.'

'Come with me,' Wright clearly chose Bodie out of all of them and started walking away. Bodie followed until the two stood next to a black railing, alone.

'We found a severed head at the crime scene,' Wright said quietly.

Bodie lost all feeling in his legs and wobbled. 'What the fu-'

'I need you to look. Show me the photo first. I can prepare you.'

There was nothing like being to the point, Bodie thought. 'But you said eight people abducted her,' he said lamely.

'They abducted someone,' Wright said. 'By the eyewitness accounts, we think it was Cassidy Coleman. But you can speed everything up by having a look right now.'

Bodie steeled himself. He let out a long breath, and then nodded. Wright led him to a white police van and knocked on the side door. It slid open immediately with a steel clunk. Bodie leaned in with Wright alongside him, the cop shouting someone's name, asking him to *bring the bag.*

Bodie took a moment to show Wright a picture of

Cassidy, taken outside the tomb they found in the Amazon, a very happy Cassidy holding one of the items they'd discovered in one hand, her red hair whipped by the wind. Wright looked at it and just grunted.

Bodie licked dry lips, suddenly glad he hadn't had breakfast that morning. The inside of the van felt claustrophobic and there was a faint odour of something gone bad. He didn't know if it was a technician's sandwich or something far worse.

One man brought a plastic box towards Bodie. It was transparent, and inside it, Bodie could make out a black garbage bag. The man then laid the box before him on the floor of the van and prised the lid off. The technician looked up at Bodie.

'You ready?'

Bodie wasn't, but nodded and braced himself. A mix of horrific feelings ran through him. He was terrified that this might be Cass, at a loss to explain why the abductors would do such a thing, scared for the person it might be. He felt revulsion, disquiet and sorrow.

The CSI reached down with gloved hands and peeled the garbage bag away from the object within. Bodie saw a shock of dark hair, a high forehead, and then a pair of hollow, staring eyes that ripped straight through him. The CSI was thoughtful, and didn't reveal the neck wound, just let Bodie stare at the face.

'That's not Cassidy,' he said, retreating.

'Thought as much,' Wright said with a slight smile. He waved at the CSI. 'Let's get on with the identification.'

Bodie backed away from the van, taking in huge gasps of air. Wright regarded him steadily.

'You okay?'

'You had to know that wasn't Cassidy. I showed you the picture.'

'Nothing like an eyewitness account,' Wright shrugged. 'Now we know one hundred per cent.'

Bodie was forced to agree that Wright was correct, but it still didn't sit well with him. He tried to force the sight of the severed head from his mind.

'Why the hell would they do that?' he asked.

'Only one answer comes to my mind,' Wright said, plucking a vape from his left jacket pocket and taking a long drag. The smoke smelled like vanilla and peach to Bodie and it stuck in his throat, sickly sweet, making him feel even more nauseous.

'Which is?' he asked.

'A warning.'

Bodie stared at him. 'A bloody warning? A *severed head?*'

Wright regarded him closely. 'You never answered my question earlier,' he said. 'Who are you people? What does Cassidy do?'

Bodie sensed a barrage of questions were coming, and he understood why. This cop had to get the clearest picture possible so that he could pursue Cassidy's abductors with all the right facts.

'Private contractors,' he said easily. 'Currently out of a job. We recently located a tomb in the Amazon containing millions of dollars' worth of treasure.'

Wright stared at him, mouth open. 'No shit,' he said eventually.

'Not even a bit. We used to work for the… government, but now we work alone.'

'Enemies?'

Bodie looked around as they sauntered back towards the team. 'Nothing clear and obvious,' he said. 'Our worst enemies are dead.'

Wright's eyes raised at that. 'Dead?'

Bodie bit his lip, realising he'd gone a little too far. 'Not by our hand,' he said. 'At least, not in a criminal way.' He could see this conversation might become incredibly tricky and convoluted so sought to change it.

'Do you have any leads?'

'All the abductors were wearing masks. All dressed in black. They torched the stolen van. Only the driver was caught on CCTV and there's not enough for facial recognition. At the moment, we're stretching.'

Bodie stopped walking as they reached the others. He didn't tell them about the head, didn't explain anything. There was no point. They looked at him expectantly.

'We're no further forward,' he said.

They looked disconsolate. Bodie looked back at Wright. 'Where do we go from here?'

'You give me your contact information and go back to your hotel. You say you're treasure hunters, well don't go hunting for anything in my backyard. Seriously. I'll keep you briefed.' Wright turned away.

'That's it?' Heidi asked. 'Hey, hey, what happened to Cassidy?'

'As I said, we're on it.'

Heidi started forward, but Bodie held her back. 'There's nothing we can do here,' he said. 'I've seen all the evidence, spoke at length with Wright. They have practically nothing.'

'We're not investigators,' Jemma said. 'What the hell are we supposed to do?'

Bodie took a long look over the crime scene. Jemma's words hit home, they hit hard. Their expertise certainly wasn't in the gathering of information relating to a police incident. He wondered if Lucie could adapt. He looked over at her.

'You're good at research,' he said. 'What can you deduce from all this?'

Lucie stared at him. 'Are you kidding? I use the internet, old files, old stories. I gather dusty old reports of ancient treasure. You're talking about a crime and a crime scene. I wouldn't know where to start.'

Bodie saw the pavement with its spots of blood, the stain where the severed head had probably landed, the place where Cassidy's phone had dropped, indicated by an A-frame yellow tent evidence marker. He cast an eye over the cop cars, the vans, the techs working the scene, now packing up. This was way beyond their scope of expertise.

'So what the hell are we going to do?' he asked, feeling hollow and small.

Heidi dug her phone from her pocket. 'Maybe I can call in a few favours,' she said.

And Bodie saw it. Of course, Heidi had a law enforcement association. Maybe she could...

His phone rang.

Bodie snatched it out of his pocket quickly, put it to his ear without checking the screen. 'Hello?'

'We have Cassidy Coleman,' a disembodied voice hissed through static. *'You will do as I say or she will die. Horribly.'*

CHAPTER FIVE

Bodie almost dropped the phone, then clasped it harder.

'What?'

'You heard me correctly, Bodie. Guy Bodie. I know you, I know all of you. Now, walk away from that crime scene so that the vaping cop doesn't overhear us.'

Bodie swallowed hard. He gave the team the hard eyes and then ducked under the crime scene tape, walking away. The pavement was still crowded with the looky-loos. He held the phone tight to his ear.

'Go on,' he said.

'Further away,' the voice said.

Bodie was incredibly unsettled, knowing that the man who had Cassidy was currently watching them. He walked along Riverside for a while until the black railings let into a small park, then walked inside.

'How about now?' he asked, conscious that the entire team were crowded around, listening.

'That'll do. Like I said, I have your friend, Cassidy.'

'How do we know that?'

'You want proof? All right then,' the voice grunted. 'Cut the bitch.'

Bodie opened his mouth to protest, but then, suddenly, there was a high-pitched cry. He heard Cassidy's scream and then her voice, promising death on the man who cut her. The voice on the other end of the phone sounded unperturbed.

'Is that enough for you, Bodie?'

He was thrown, taken aback. This guy had Cassidy and wasn't afraid to hurt her. He had called Bodie by name, as if they were colleagues. Above, the sun shone down, and the wind was warm; the day was turning out to be quite balmy, but it was anything but for the relic hunters.

'Put her on the phone,' Bodie tried.

'Not a chance. She's unharmed, mostly. I must say, the more time that passes, the less likely it is to stay that way. She's a bitch. Makes me want to chop into her. You'd better hurry, Bodie.'

He wished the asshole would stop saying his name. 'Hurry? What do you mean?'

'You're going to meet me. Central Park at noon. No cops, or your precious Cassidy gets what she deserves – a cold harsh blade to the throat. Are you listening?'

'I hear you.'

'No fucking cops. Repeat that back to me.'

'I said I hear you.'

'That's great, Bodie, just great. My name's LaRoy, by the way. Now we're friends.'

Bodie said nothing.

The man named LaRoy gave Bodie directions. 'There's a bench,' he said. 'Black with gilt edges. It sits off West Drive directly behind the Dakota. Can't miss it when you get close. Don't be late.'

The line went dead. Bodie swallowed, looked at his phone. There was no number, no caller ID. He looked around at the others.

'They kidnapped Cassidy because of us,' he said. 'Because of the relic hunters.'

Heidi checked her watch. 'It's ten thirty,' she said. 'We'd better head over to Central Park right away. Find this damn bench.'

Bodie agreed. Central Park was huge, and he had no idea where the Dakota was, or even *what* it was at this point. He hesitated for a moment. Nobody seemed to know what to say. Bodie felt trapped, responsible. He wished they'd thought more about security, but knew nobody was to blame. The job they did, he guessed, actually made them targets to all scumbags at all times.

Time ticked slowly by. They headed east, passing their hotel and then the Museum of Natural History that backed onto Central Park. They found a way into the vast green expanse and started walking along the various pathways. Lucie brought up the Dakota on Google Maps and led the way towards it.

'The Dakota is an old apartment building,' she told them as they walked. 'Built between 1880 and 1884. It's unique when compared to the surrounding buildings, constructed in the Renaissance Revival style.'

'Well, we shouldn't miss it,' Reilly said.

Bodie nodded. 'According to this,' he nodded at his own phone. 'We're not far away.'

By 11.15 they had located the bench and were walking away from it. Lucie found them a refreshment stand, and they bought coffee, tea and pastries, since none of them had eaten breakfast and they were all famished. They found two benches together and sat there, eating and drinking in silence. Bodie felt the much-needed caffeine hit his system and went back to the stand to order another.

Time marched on. Together, they didn't say much. They thought only of LaRoy and what he might want with them. Bodie didn't like to think too deeply at this point – all the harsh roads kept leading back to Cassidy's predicament.

At 11.50 he rose and made his way across to the

black and gilt bench that stood behind the Dakota. The sun shone down harshly on his skull, on the nape of his neck. He was angry, nervous, scared. His stomach churned. The bench was empty.

Bodie sat down heavily on it, scooted to one end. Ahead, a few flat patches of green were bordered by thick green hedges and low trees. There was a road in the distance that cut through Central Park, probably West Drive. People came and went, strolling through the expanse, many with dogs and prams and some walking hand in hand. It was a relaxed atmosphere, a sight that unnerved Bodie even more.

A figure approached. Bodie shielded his eyes. The man approaching wore a black suit and had shiny shoes. Bodie rose, now able to make the figure out better. The face was narrow, the eyes ringed by dark circles. Bodie blinked. The guy had no eyebrows, none at all. He approached with a self-satisfied smirk on his face.

'Guy Bodie,' he said, sitting straight down. 'The man who's going to beg to work for me.'

'Is Cassidy okay?'

'She's bleeding. She's bruised. She's cranky as hell. How do you put up with her?'

Bodie saw a superior quality radiating from the man sitting next to him. The guy regarded himself as a cut above the rest. He already knew the asshole was vicious, and now confirmed the arrogance. 'She'd best be in good health,' he growled.

'Oh, she's kicking and squealing like an untamed horse,' LaRoy grinned. 'We were thinking of sending her back to you broken. Tamed. Would you like that?'

Bodie's hands curled into fists. He half rose, then got a hold of himself and sat back down. He bit his bottom lip until the blood flowed.

Hierarchy of Madness

'Tell me what the fuck you want.'

'Of course, my friend, of course. That's why we're here, why good old Cassidy was taken in the first place. That wasn't easy, by the way. I'm so glad I over compensated with my men. She pretty much took them all out before they rallied.' LaRoy's laughter filled the spaces between them.

'Speak now,' Bodie grated.

'All right then. My name is LaRoy, as you know. I am what you might call a wealthy eccentric. I have money, lots of it but, unfortunately, money can't solve my current problems.' The black suited man crossed his shiny shoes.

'You want my help.' Bodie said flatly. It wasn't a question.

'Oh, I want all your help. The famous — or should that be *in*famous relic hunters? Your reputation precedes you. I know what you did in the Amazon, the impossible clues you followed to get there. I know what you can do.'

'How the hell could you know any of that? We only just told our story to the government, and it was all classified.'

'Don't be so naïve. That you told the government should start the alarm bells ringing. They don't have the best reputation for honesty, you know.'

Bodie gave him that one. He held the man's eyes. 'I want an update on Cassidy.'

'Yes, yes, I thought as much,' LaRoy felt inside his pocket for something, found it and brought it out. Bodie saw a mobile device.

LaRoy gave it to him. 'Press the video icon and then play.'

Bodie swallowed. For LaRoy, this was all about

power. For Bodie, it was about survival. He pressed play and watched the screen.

It was unfocused at first, just a blur of colour. Then the camera resolved onto a set of four iron bars across a window, like a prison cell. It travelled down a pitted, stained wall until it landed on a pair of black training shoes, then some leggings, and then the stomach of a woman. The camera moved slowly, as if savouring what was to come. It took its time wandering across the woman's upper half and then, draped across the shoulders, Bodie saw the red hair. Finally, Cassidy's face came into view.

'She got injured during the fight,' LaRoy was watching and shrugging.

Cassidy's face was bruised and bloody, her hair matted in red, but she glared at the camera with a ferocity Bodie knew all about. She didn't look cowed or beaten; quite the opposite. Cassidy was a wild animal waiting to be unleashed.

The camera went on to show a copy of today's New York Times sat on the floor next to Cassidy's bed.

'You have your proof,' LaRoy snatched the device away and thrust it back into his pocket. 'Now you will listen to me-'

'Wait,' Bodie said, holding up a hand. 'I don't get it. Why the severed head?'

LaRoy let out a bark of genuine humour. 'Oh, that. Don't you get it? It was a warning. Don't fuck with us... or else. Plus, of course, it was fun.'

Bodie stared at him, shook his head slightly. 'Fun?'

LaRoy grinned. 'You have a lot to learn about my family. Are you ready?'

Bodie looked away from the man, stared at the park, the hedges and the greenery, the content people sitting and walking and enjoying their day, the strobes of diffused sunlight that pierced a nearby stand of trees. Was this all real? Or a nightmare?

'Are you listening, Bodie? I need your help. You remember I told you how wealthy and eccentric I am? Well, the eccentric part is right. Unfortunately, my money is currently haemorrhaging. It's pouring away faster than water through a broken dam. Companies are tottering, an empire is floundering. Have you heard of my family name before?'

Bodie shook his head.

'LaRoy is old money, made on the railroads and oil. We were part of the American revolution,' he laughed. 'Anyway, our blood has become somewhat polluted over the centuries. Or should I say – infected? We're a bit of a mad bunch, I'm afraid to say. And none more insane than my father.'

LaRoy paused and then swallowed hard. 'You wouldn't want to meet him,' he said.

Bodie let out a sigh. 'To be honest, I don't really want to meet you.'

'Of course, Bodie. Of course. But be respectful. I have something of yours that you need back in one piece. Now, I am very rich, very influential. If I want something done, I have the contacts to get it done. But one thing I can't do is to influence my own extended family.'

Bodie shook his head. 'I don't get it.'

'You will. I need something from my family. I need it bad. And Bodie, they're unlikely to want to give it up. You see, they're all quite mad.'

'You want me to squeeze blood from madmen?'

'Of course I want you too. And believe me when I say: Cassidy's fingers, toes, eyelids, her very life depends on it.'

CHAPTER SIX

There were people everywhere, strolling, jogging, walking with canes and prams and strollers and frames. They were chatting, laughing, even singing. The sun shone on them.

Bodie saw none of it. Though bathed in light, he sat in the shadow of darkness and evil.

LaRoy laughed when he talked of murdering Cassidy. He licked his lips, eyes shining. Though he talked about his family's madness, Bodie could see the taint was firmly fastened to him, too.

Fastened like a second skin.

Bodie listened. The man's story was incredulous.

'My father, the crazy bastard, had seven children. Three girls and four boys. Yes, it's a large family, but the rich had nothing to do but procreate in those days. And we had nannies, butlers, servants if you like, to take care of the nastier things.' He made a point of lowering his voice, leaning in to Bodie and whispering: *'I still do.'*

And then he laughed uproariously.

Bodie swallowed, easing himself away from the man. 'Go on.'

'You're warming to me, I can tell. Anyway, these seven children grew up to be seven maladjusted adults, some far worse than others. Honestly, I am the by far the sanest one of them all. Nothing wrong with me, thank God.'

HIERARCHY OF MADNESS

'Is there a point to this?' Bodie asked.

'Of course. A very sharp point. It all revolves around the family wealth. My father... he played a fine joke on us.'

'A joke?'

'Yes, yes, it didn't seem pertinent at the time. You see, we all had our share of wealth. All had quite a bit of it, to be honest. That prevented jealousy, infighting, all the rest of it. But my father was such a crazy old fool. He amassed vast amounts of wealth in old family heirlooms.'

Bodie didn't get it, and how it related to him. 'Heirlooms?'

'Yes, you heard me correctly. Heirlooms in the form of gemstones. You know what gemstones are?'

Bodie felt affronted at being asked. 'Diamonds, gold, jade, amber... you name it. Precious stones.'

'You got it. Gemstones. Millions of dollars' worth. So, one cold, windy night, with the fires blowing and flurrying in the hearth, he sat us all down in the drawing room and told us a story. Though we were but fifteen to twenty-one, he furnished us all with spirits, with plates of meat and fish, with a notebook each. Standing tall, he stoked the fire, looked us all in the eye, and then proceeded to explain that the family wealth was strong, it was vast, and he'd worked hard to keep it that way. He explained how he would divvy some of it up between us, an equal share, and that we would never, ever, get another penny. The man didn't want us working for him, for his companies. He wanted us gone as soon as possible because he thought we were all liabilities. Mad idiots, he called us.'

'Sounds like a great guy,' Bodie said.

'Oh, we're not done there, not by any means. We ate,

and we drank and we listened as my father told us this crazy tale. I'll never forget it. There were shadows in the hearth, shadows on the walls, thrown there by the raging flames, all dancing and capering like wild demons. My memory is full of the terror and impossibility of that night. As the demons cavorted, my father told us he'd put a huge chunk of his fortune into the family heirlooms. And that he'd hidden them away. He then proceeded to give us, all seven of us, one line to what he called the Stanza – the LaRoy Family Stanza – a group of lines that would lead the way to the gemstones.'

Bodie's mouth had dropped open. He blinked. 'Are you kidding?'

'It was a fabulous joke for him. He knew half of us were mad, half of us insane, that we all hated each other, and that we could *never* get together and use the lines as they were meant to be used. My father was the cruellest, meanest man I have ever known. He took great delight in revealing this new family fortune to his children, and then engineering it so they could never touch it.'

'Let me get this straight,' Bodie said. 'First, your father amassed a fortune in precious gemstones. Then he hid all this wealth somewhere. Later, he revealed that fact to his kids, and then boasted that they could never lay their hands on the stones because they weren't sane enough to work together?'

LaRoy shrugged. 'He was quite mad.'

'You don't say.'

'The LaRoy family name is tinged with madness all the way from the beginning. My old grandmother tied herself to the front of a train she owned and threatened the driver that if he didn't drive it at full speed, she would ruin him. All this to catch the eye of the man she loved. My great grandfather drove his car into a lake and drowned to piss his wife off. My uncle once shot nine of our horses because one "looked at him funny." There isn't a sane bone between them.'

'I'm starting to see that,' Bodie said.

'Then you understand that what my father did was the cruellest act imaginable.'

'He couldn't have known your wealth would run out,' Bodie said.

LaRoy eyed him and then spread his hand. 'Um, *mad,*' he said. 'Of course he knew the wealth would run out. He delighted in knowing it and that, one day, we would all come to remember the hidden family heirlooms.'

'And you are the first,' Bodie said.

'What?'

'I assume you're the first to remember the old heirlooms, to want to search for them?'

LaRoy nodded. 'I have one line,' he said. 'Of the Stanza. I need you to get me the other six.'

Bodie pursed his lips. 'That's not what we do. Maybe when you get all seven lines, and then have to search for the... treasure.'

LaRoy slapped the bench in anger. 'No! I want you to get all the lines. I don't care how you do it. One isn't enough. Two isn't enough. *Six* isn't enough! I want all seven!'

It was a fit of rage, a tantrum that shouldn't have surprised Bodie. LaRoy was visibly unstable. Bodie feared for Cassidy's longevity. What the hell was he supposed to do?

'You have a business empire of your own?' he asked, primarily to calm the mad fucker down.

'Yes, yes, Bodie, I do. A vast conflagration of ideals. I hit rough waves years ago, tried to keep everything afloat. It's a harsh, cutthroat industry is pharmaceuticals. You take shortcuts, the bastards always get you later.'

'You mean after innocent civilians die?'

'Whatever. That's not the point here. The point is, you work for me now until I tell you otherwise. Cassidy is mine. *You* are mine. I hope you understand that, and I want you to say it.'

Bodie fought down a sudden urge to slap this guy even sillier. He looked up at the blue sky, took a deep breath, and then turned back to LaRoy.

'I am yours. I will help as much as I am able.'

'Say it like you mean it.'

'For God's sake, I-'

'Ha, ha, I'm kidding. That will do for now. I'll think of something else later. Now, remember, I know your team. Jemma. Lucie. Yasmine. Heidi. And the other guy, Reilly. Don't you try to fool me, Bodie.'

'Any ideas what these gemstones are? What kind of size we're talking about?'

LaRoy regarded him with interest. 'I see your mind working. That's good. Gemstones are the earth's most beautiful natural treasures, appreciated through the years for very different reasons. Alongside beauty, with gemstones comes avarice and danger and jealousy and violence. Doesn't matter what the beauty is. They attract a complex mix of emotions. Some gemstones are known for their religious symbolism, even for healing powers. But some gems are rarer than others. You have Tanzanite at over $1,200 per carat, Black Opal at over $10,000. There's ruby and diamonds and jadeite in the millions. And then there are the rarest – Taaffite, Red

Beryl, Benitoite. You can be sure my father included many of them.'
'And the size?'
'Big. An entire chest full of it.'
'Any ideas where he might hide or bury it?'
LaRoy shook his head. 'My father owns property all over America. Thousands of places. Who knows?'
'And you're sure none of your siblings found it?'
LaRoy guffawed. 'Are you kidding? They're all loonier than a bag of snakes.'
Bodie thought about that for a moment. This coming from a man who severed heads and then laughed about it, who abducted women to further his own needs and then threatened to maim them, who hailed from a hierarchy of madness.
'What's your line?' he asked suddenly.
LaRoy shifted on the bench, uncrossing his legs and recrossing them the other way. Bodie still hadn't got used to the lack of eyebrows as he fixed his gaze on the man. LaRoy cleared his throat.
'A Ghost Town famous in the nineteenth century,' he said.
Bodie waited for more, but nothing was forthcoming. 'Is that it?'
'Exactly the problem.'
'How many ghost towns were famous in the nineteenth century?'
'Hundreds. I've checked. And, if read properly, it could mean a ghost town *now,* but famous in the nineteenth century.'
Bodie knew he was right. 'Weren't they all the gold rush towns?'
'Yeah, and there are countless ones across America.'
'And there are six other verses to this stanza, and you need all six?'

'You're getting there, Bodie.'

'What makes you think your brothers and sisters will want to give them to me?'

LaRoy gestured angrily. 'I don't care how you get them, just *get them,* and fast. Precious Cassidy's continued health depends on it. She can't stay locked up forever.'

That was true at least, Bodie thought. Cassidy was wild, not meant to be caged. 'Is she close?' he asked.

'You will never find her. Don't let your focus veer from the task at hand. If you deviate or fail, she dies.'

Bodie nodded, a little sick of hearing the same old threats. He knew what was at stake better than the mad bastard sitting next to him.

'You'd better tell me about your siblings,' he said.

CHAPTER SEVEN

'And there you have a great story,' LaRoy said. 'As I mentioned, I have three brothers and three sisters. Some are almost sane, others are far from it. I've kept close tabs on them all, even though they never returned the favour. Shall I start with my favourite? Yes, I'll start with my favourite.' he took a deep breath.

LaRoy then removed something from his inside jacket pocket and handed it to Bodie. 'You will need this folder. It contains information on all six of my siblings. It's thick and detailed, and holds everything you need to know and everything I'm about to tell you. First, you have the serial killer.'

Bodie swallowed hard. 'The what?'

'Yes, I'm afraid Antonio became a serial killer. It wasn't a surprise, though. He used to harm small animals, you know? Always was a bastard,' LaRoy laughed so hard he choked. 'Anyway,' he continued when he'd got hold of himself. 'Antonio killed eight people up and down the spine of the U.S. And they never found the heads, just the bodies buried in marshland.'

'They never found the... heads?' Bodie reiterated.

'Oh, no. Some say Antonio ate them.' LaRoy shrugged. 'Doesn't really matter. Antonio is currently incarcerated in a supermax prison. Been there for ten years.'

Bodie opened his mouth to speak, but no words came out.

LaRoy continued. 'Next up is the lunatic. And I mean, a real, proper lunatic. Leanne is in a mental institution, locked away for years. She graduated from shoplifting to harassment and then to bodily harm of one of her boyfriends. Then she assaulted a police officer, badly, and should have gone to prison, but the family has influence and, instead, they sent her to a sanitorium.'

'I'm finding this a little hard to follow,' Bodie said.

'She sees things. Bats. Birds. Rattlesnakes. Who the fuck cares? Leanne's crazy as all shit and no mistake. She has her lucid moments, though, few and far between. I suggest you choose one of those.'

LaRoy was grinning widely as he went on. 'Third, I give you the recluse, Gary. Now Gary has gone and shunned society, well... life really. He's never seen, never heard from. You need to track him down. I have a vague idea of where he's at. But Gary will hate seeing you, make no mistake. And, oh, he loves guns.' Another cackle.

'Fourth, we have the jet setter. Now Paulina is a party-goer, a flasher of wealth, a socialite. She's totally self-centred, sees herself as the centre of the universe. Seriously, nothing else matters. Not people's lives, feelings, emotions. Paulina can't see beyond herself. She has no morals, no ethics, cares for no one. She *can't* feel. But she's loaded, and everyone forgives her for being such a cold, heartless bitch, obviously.'

Bodie sat back. 'At least she sounds relatively normal.'

'She isn't. But let me finish. We're on the fifth of my dear brothers and sisters now. Here we have little old

Stuart. The Collector. Keeps everything under lock and key. He's paranoid to the extreme and hates other humans so much that, if they come near him, he threatens to kill them. What a guy, eh? He once shot at a car that went the wrong way up his drive. He lives alone, with alarms, and God knows what else. You will have your work cut out with that one, Bodie.'

'And let's have the sixth then.'

'Oh, the sixth? Well, her name is Anna, but I call her the Body Snatcher.'

Bodie couldn't help but close his eyes once more. He shook his head in disbelief. 'Go on.'

'Kimberley was once convicted of digging up old bodies to experiment on. She went to jail and is actually out now, living a quiet life. But she will help anyone who offers her an interesting diversion. Perhaps you can think of something.'

'Bodies to experiment on?' Bodie repeated.

'Experiment on... make sweet love to... whatever,' LaRoy's eyes sparkled with laughter. 'That's the lot. What do you think?'

'I think you're asking for the impossible. Do you have any other ideas?'

LaRoy stopped smiling right then, and his face looked like mid-winter. 'I think you need to explain yourself.'

'We're good,' Bodie said. 'We can do almost anything. But we can't get into supermax's, into lunatic asylums, and then question the inmates. We can't go that far.'

LaRoy nodded in understanding. 'I understand that. Haven't you been listening? I told you my family has influence, lots of it from the time of my father and grandfather and even before that. I can get you into the supermax, into the mental institution. Yes, I can arrange the visitation rights.'

'And the others? The jet setter, the recluse, the bloody collector?'

'Those you will have to handle yourself.'

'I'm assuming you have had no contact with any of your siblings?'

'Are you kidding? They're stark raving lunatics.'

Bodie bit his tongue, about to say something he'd probably regret. 'I don't know where to begin,' he said.

'Then find a spot and stick a pin in it. Because I want all six lines in one week.'

Bodie felt the world closing in. 'One week? That's impossible. The travel times at least will...'

'Okay, take as long as you wish,' LaRoy said. 'But after one week I start cutting off digits and mailing them to the New York Times. How does that sound to you?'

It was then that the other relic hunters started materialising out of the park. Bodie never knew if they did it for solidarity, to intimidate, to show LaRoy they were a team, or for some other reason, but he welcomed it. He was floundering, awash with dreadful information and a terrible purpose, and he needed all the help he could get. He watched them as they approached.

'Your team,' LaRoy said.

My family, Bodie wanted to say, but didn't. Cassidy was a part of that family. He didn't want to give LaRoy any more ammunition than was necessary, didn't want him to get the idea to nab another of his friends, just for leverage.

Jemma arrived first, then Heidi, Yasmine and Lucie. Finally, Reilly came up behind them, standing slightly apart. Together, they all faced LaRoy.

'And what a wonderful meeting,' he said. 'My new team, assembled together.'

'Don't you dare hurt Cassidy,' Heidi warned him. 'Or you'll have all of us to answer to.'

'She will suffer no lasting damage for the next week,' LaRoy said.

Bodie wondered exactly what that was supposed to mean. Lucie spoke up next. 'Whatever you need,' she said. 'If it has anything to do with research, I can help.'

'Oh, you will have all the research you can handle.'

Jemma stepped up. 'You have one of the best teams in the world here,' she said. 'Tried and tested. Be assured, if we want to get to you, we will.'

'I understand and urge you to save the life of your friend. Don't test me.'

Bodie stood up, holding the thick folder in his right hand. He was sweating, and didn't know if it was because of the direct sunlight or the size of the task in front of them. Before he could move, Reilly stepped forward.

'I'm new here,' he said. 'But I can tell you this. I'm a smuggler, a criminal, and I have a criminal background. I survived the Amazon rainforest, the drug dealers, the gunrunners, the cutthroats. I ran with the Bratva. Yeah, I know I'm pretty, but that's all on the outside. Cassidy is my friend too. If anything happens to her, anything at all, I will use all of my considerable skills to rip your fucking head off.'

Bodie winced. He was grateful for Reilly's words, but wasn't sure how LaRoy would take them. To be fair, LaRoy's decision-making capabilities and reactions changed with every alternating gust of wind.

'Just do as I have commanded. You will earn her freedom.'

LaRoy looked up at them.

'Time's a-wasting.'

Bodie looked down at him. 'The supermax? The mental institute?'

'Ah, I have arranged the supermax for tomorrow, the sanitorium for the day after. They're close enough. Does that suit?'

Bodie nodded and listened to the details. They would have no problem getting in and out and, fortunately, neither facility was too far away. Two days gone left five to sort out the other four family members.

'How do we keep in touch?' he asked.

LaRoy threw him a burner phone. 'It's programmed with just one number,' he said. 'Mine.'

Bodie pocketed the device and turned away. 'Any advice with your brethren?' he asked finally.

LaRoy grinned from ear to ear. 'Treat them as lunatics,' he said. 'They'll enjoy that. You see, my father told us for years that we were irrational, absurd, one pack short of a full load. He drummed it into us. I think he wanted unsound children, and look what he got. My father hated us, did everything he could to undermine our future. It was all a game to him. See which one he could damage the most. Bodie, if you talk to them about madness, they will know exactly what you mean.'

Bodie nodded, not trusting himself to speak to the guy any further. It was a long time before he felt calm enough to explain their predicament to his team.

CHAPTER EIGHT

LaRoy adjusted his suit jacket until it hung just right, checked the shine of his patented black shoes and gazed at himself briefly in the car's tinted window. All looked fine. He had been a little nervous meeting up with the relic hunters alone, but had also been relatively certain nothing would happen. Holding their friend captive helped embolden that assumption and awful lot.

LaRoy climbed into the car, pressed the engine button and smiled to hear the Cadillac's five litre engine burst into life. He had men watching the car and was confident nobody had followed him.

LaRoy reviewed the facts as he drove. Bodie and co were on board. They were top-notch at what they did. Somehow, they would find a way to coax those lines out of his brethren. They really had no other choice. Speaking of his siblings, LaRoy reviewed them in his head. The serial killer. The Lunatic. The Recluse. The Jet Setter. The Collector. The Body Snatcher. That was how he'd presented them, and it had taken him some considerable time to come up with those descriptions. He'd kept close tabs on them through the years, always wondering if, at some point, he might need one of them.

Or need to *use* one of them.

LaRoy thought about his business, the ruin that it

had become. Of course, nobody knew yet. If they did, they'd desert him faster than rats deserting a sinking ship. He was on the edge, waiting to fall.

And fall... and fall...

The traffic hemmed him in on all sides, spoiling his journey. LaRoy saw nothing but a sea of red lights along Park Avenue. At this rate, it would take him hours to reach home. With that thought in his mind, LaRoy tapped a number into the car phone app.

'It's me,' he said when the call picked up. 'How's our visitor?'

The man on the other end of the line was named Friday. An odd nickname, born out of the fact that, in a previous existence, he always rang in sick on a Friday. The name had stuck. Friday kind of liked it.

'Belligerent, boss. Aggressive. But tired, hungry, thirsty. She looks good in chains.'

'She's still fighting?' LaRoy felt surprise.

'With every breath she takes.'

LaRoy braked suddenly to avoid an idiot jaywalker crossing the road, the guy sauntering along as if oblivious to the presence of cars. 'I think you should feed and water her.'

'Are you kidding, boss? The way she is... she'll take my hand off. Probably eat it.'

LaRoy knew Friday was jesting. The guy was loyal and would never gainsay his boss. 'Be careful,' he said easily.

'I'll get young Friedman to do it. He's expendable.'

LaRoy hadn't given much thought on how to feed and water a cantankerous, feral prisoner. He did now, moving along in the stop-start traffic. 'I guess you'd better unchain one hand. That should work. We don't want her to croak on us.'

'At least, not yet,' Friday laughed.

'Describe her to me.' It didn't really bother him who they had in captivity, man or woman, but he liked the thought of them under his control.

LaRoy sat back in lascivious comfort, listening as Friday first described what Cassidy was wearing, the state of her cuts and bruises, and then the clothes that covered her body. He liked the description of how her chains fit her wrists and ankles, how the collar gripped her slender neck. He licked his lips when Friday came to the long red hair. How they tied it in clumps to the wall to hold her in place.

'And how does Cassidy hold up to a beating?' he asked.

Friday laughed once more, clearly enjoying himself. 'We haven't started anything in earnest yet, just a few slaps here and there. But, yeah, she's a feisty one. I'd hate to come up against her one on one with no manacles.'

'Apparently, she's trained.'

'Yeah, you can tell. Has all the right muscles in all the right places. Holds herself well even in captivity. Good reactions. Doesn't show pain. You'd think her nerves were shot.'

LaRoy saw an end to the rows of red lights ahead. They looked to be past the worst of it. 'I should be back in an hour. Get Friedman to feed her before I get back. I want to talk to her, find out what makes her tick before we break her down.'

'I'm guessing the meeting went well, boss?'

'Perfectly. I promised them Cassidy Coleman back in one piece if they come through, but I didn't say she'd be the same person.'

'Excellent.'

LaRoy ended the call, thought about what lay ahead. He couldn't relax. The hammer looming over his life hung ominously, poised to fall. The fact was, he needed the relic hunters, needed them to come through. Yet, he still couldn't deny himself a bit of delicious fun with the captive. He loved to watch them break – the men and women he chose to work on. That Cassidy was a strong-willed, hard-bodied individual only served to entice him even more.

LaRoy forced her from his mind. There were other things to consider. He recalled his own line of the Stanza, the very first line as it happened.

A Ghost Town famous in the nineteenth century.

Six more to come, he thought. He hoped to God they were more revealing than his own. The family heirloom was all important, the glorious chest of gemstones. If he could just find it, all his problems would be in the past. He'd be solvent again. A player. And most important – he'd be able to carry on his lifestyle as if nothing had happened.

LaRoy pondered on the craziness of his family. It hadn't started with his father, of course. There were mad bastards well before him. But his father had definitely passed the trait on to his kids, and with intent and enthusiasm. When LaRoy looked back, it felt as though his father had ensured the family trait lived on. The way he'd treated his kids had been abominable.

LaRoy couldn't think about his father without remembering his mother. In a terrifying twist, it was said that their father had murdered their mother. It was even said that their mother was buried somewhere on the family estate that LaRoy now owned. That idea, that possibility, gnawed at LaRoy's mind like a savage rat. The thought of looking out over that estate day after day, night after night, knowing...

Hierarchy of Madness

He shrugged it away. It wouldn't do him any good. LaRoy knew it could never be proven. Still, the family was notorious for its *eccentricity*, a polite way of saying *madness*. From the father to the sons and daughters, the whole damn hierarchy.

LaRoy drove carefully, keeping the car under the speed limits. The last thing he wanted at the moment was attention from the cops. He passed through the outer gates with their high walls and crunched up a twisting gravel driveway. The house came into sight, a rambling mansion with ivy up the walls and leaded windows, red-tiled gables and double-height doors. It had about as much conformity as a lunatic's pencil drawing and carried with it the personality of his father.

LaRoy left the car where it was and entered the house. A man wearing a shoulder holster took his coat and hung it up. LaRoy walked to his study, poured himself a large, stiff drink and downed it before pouring another. For a moment, he walked across to the window and looked out over the grounds, thinking of his mother. It was finely sculpted out there, tended by a groundskeeper. There were rolling hills and flower-filled mounds and stands of trees, all neatly clipped. LaRoy guessed that would do it for some people. It didn't do it for him. He finished his drink, poured one more. He was looking forward to what came next, savouring the anticipation.

Soon, he headed down to the cells.

There were more of his men down here, all wearing shoulder holsters and t-shirts that clung tight to their chests. They laughed together and drank beverages and took phone calls, helping to run his empire. Not one of them – including Friday, his most trusted employee –

knew of the financial difficulties... the overlying pile of shit that threatened them. Nobody knew except LaRoy.

The cells lay at the very lowest level of the mansion. It was cold down here, cold and damp and airless. Seeing his men scattered about made LaRoy consider his entire organisation. He had fifty or sixty men working for him, drawing a wage, and had a small criminal enterprise going on the side. This was in addition to the normal business dealings, the pharmaceutical crap – as he thought of it – and the dabbling's in the oil reserves. It was a finely tuned machine, an entity LaRoy had been lauding over for many years.

But truth be told, he loved the criminal side of it. The badness tapped into that side of him that was entirely crazy.

The first cell was almost empty. LaRoy did a double take when he saw Friday sitting inside, legs crossed, scrolling through his phone.

'What the hell?'

'Ah, boss,' Friday jumped up. 'Just taking a breather. Had to help Friedman get himself cleaned up.'

'Cleaned up?'

'That Cassidy bitch did a good number on him. It's as though she doesn't want to be fed and watered. Let him remove a chain and then got him by the throat, squeezed. Slapped him. Punched him. Squeezed again. It took three of us to get him the hell out of there.'

LaRoy liked it. 'I see. She is indeed a fighter. Is she properly chained now?'

Friday let out a deep breath. 'Finally,' he said.

'Approachable?'

'That depends, boss.'

'On what?'

'On how long you want to live,' Friday guffawed, then cleared his throat. 'No, really, you should be fine.'

LaRoy hesitated. Friday's words had resurrected another problem in his mind. Something big. LaRoy employed a lot of men and women; he even employed a lot of *evil* men and women. He didn't trust any of them. But he was *forced* to trust his top three henchmen. That would be Friday, Hirsch and Braun. Those three doled out his orders, saw to his more personal needs, made sure the businesses were running smoothly. LaRoy hated it, but he had no choice but to trust these three men. It didn't sit well with LaRoy.

And he was sure at least one of them was working against him.

He couldn't be sure, couldn't pin down the concern. They were often together, working as one, working to overcome some problem or other. LaRoy was reasonably confident about Friday – it was the other two that worried him. Hirsch was one of those quiet but functional sorts, not phased by anything. Braun was confrontational and brash and in-your-face. It was a good mix.

But something was off. And these three men knew all about his business. They were inside every last detail of it.

LaRoy saw that something wasn't right in the stance of his men, their conversations, their reactions to him. He knew that someone was passing privileged information on. Thank god, he thought, that nobody knew of the financial difficulties. They'd probably string him up by his heels.

Friday, Hirsch and Braun. They knew he wanted to force the relic hunters to find the family heirlooms, but they didn't know exactly why. The men thought it was a whim, one-upmanship, greed. They thought he was trying to get one over on his family, belittle his father. It was a good, believable front.

The problem was that Friday, Hirsch and Braun now knew about the family gemstones.

Telling them had been a risk LaRoy just had to take. And maybe... just maybe... the knowledge would force the traitor to show his hand.

LaRoy tried not to think about that as Friday approached him. But it was hard not to envision one of his men cheating him. Maybe even now plotting to grab the family gemstones, plotting against LaRoy.

Was he paranoid? Was it the madness seeping through his brain?

No, it's real. I know it's real.

He didn't trust his three generals. No, he *knew* one of them was working against him. Paranoia had nothing to do with it. LaRoy would flush them out, and then he'd make an example of them, hurt them badly.

'Where is she?' he asked.

'Cell five, boss.'

'Why cell five?'

'It's the most secure.'

Good point. La Roy took a deep breath, finished the drink that was still in his hand, and then started walking up the aisle between cells, fixing a harsh smile to his face. He was ready to meet this woman, this wildcat, this killer, the figure that put the fear of God into his most valued men.

Something festering inside him wanted to eat her alive.

'Cassidy Coleman,' he said upon sighting her. 'I am the man who is going to break you.'

CHAPTER NINE

Bodie wasn't surprised that it took LaRoy the best part of the next day to get special dispensation for them to visit the serial killer, Antonio LaRoy, but he was surprised when he found out that the meeting could be conducted even in the dead of night.

Hours passed without a word. Then, finally, at four o'clock, LaRoy rang the burner phone he'd given them and told them to get to upstate New York. It didn't matter how long it would take to reach the prison. A visit with Antonio LaRoy was ensured at any time of day.

Bodie had already hired a car. They piled in, negotiated the tricky central New York traffic and were soon heading north towards Franklin County. The supermax up there had been open for twenty years and housed some of the U.S.'s worst criminals.

They stopped for food and drink and to gas the car up. They undertook the drive in relative silence; the team had already talked themselves out discussing LaRoy and Cassidy's disappearance and what alternatives they had. None of them wanted to trust the police to find Cassidy first. None of them preferred telling the cops about LaRoy, about the meeting in Central Park. That wasn't the way to get Cassidy back unharmed.

But neither was this, Bodie thought.

Doing the madman's bidding. The obvious way out of this was to find the gemstones first. Then they'd have leverage. And finding lost treasures was what the relic hunters excelled at.

They drove on as the day slipped into night. The sun soon fell below the western horizon, its last rays painting the landscape crimson and throwing shadows across Bodie's face in the driving seat.

'Feels kind of weird,' Heidi said once. 'Driving through the dark to see a serial killer in prison.'

'It's surreal,' Bodie said. 'Not the kind of thing we're used to.'

The chatter fell flat. They were all feeling it. There was a sense of losing control, of rushing into the unknown. LaRoy's story of his father, his family, his siblings was as crazy as its participants. In the backseat, Lucie had taken it upon herself to research Antonio LaRoy and all the terrible things he'd done.

'This guy murdered eight people ten years ago,' she said. 'And, unfortunately, yes, they never found the heads. It happened in New York itself; the bodies being found in the rail yards, abandoned tenement buildings and alongside the docks. Obviously, Antonio's calling card was the lack of a head. The killing spree lasted three months, a body every couple of weeks, and the detective in charge resigned at the end of it all.'

'Does it say why?' Yasmine asked.

'Not exactly. The paper drew its own conclusions. They say Detective Demetris saw evil in Antonio LaRoy, pure evil. Something so wicked he'd never encountered it in thirty years on the force. It affected him so badly he resigned. They say Detective Demetris never spoke about the murders again, not to anyone. It literally destroyed him.'

The miles flashed beneath them. The night drew in until utter blackness blanketed the landscapes outside. Bodie guided the car through intersections and junctions and down more than a few winding back roads. Eventually they came in sight of the supermax and, at night, its high-walled structure was alight. The closer you got, the brighter it became until Bodie approached the front gates and stopped the car to use an intercom.

'Guy Bodie to see Antonio LaRoy,' he spoke into it, assured by LaRoy that that would do the trick.

Sure enough, the gates were unlocked and started sliding open with a heavy clunking sound. A couple of guards oversaw the process and then waved Bodie through. He drove up a winding hill before turning right into a large parking area. At this time of night, the place was all but deserted, apart from the staff parking.

'It's gone midnight,' Heidi said.

'We'll have the place to ourselves,' Lucie said.

'Oh, yeah, apart from a few thousand dangerous inmates who wouldn't hesitate to cut our throats,' Jemma said.

'You'd feel better breaking in?' Bodie asked the cat burglar.

'Surprisingly, no.'

'Has anyone given thought to how we're going to approach this?' Reilly asked then. So far, during the journey, he'd been taciturn.

'A damn good question,' Bodie said. 'I guess it depends how Antonio reacts to us.'

They approached the front doors, waited for someone to open them. Inside they crossed a lobby that reminded Bodie of a medical corridor, all shiny, beige surfaces and the sharp smell of cleanliness. They approached a counter at the far side that could have been a hotel reception desk.

Again, Bodie spoke the magic words. The guy on the desk, a rotund, bearded fellow, tapped a few words into his computer and then started nodding.

'You must have some juice, bud. Says here you got twenty-four-hour access.'

'That's why we're here,' Bodie said.

'Well, good luck. From what I hear, the guy you're gonna see's a real piece of work.'

'What do you know about that?' Lucie asked, interested.

'Oh, nothing much. Just chatter among the guards. Antonio LaRoy's a serial killer and he knows it. Treats it like an accolade, if you know what I mean. If you offered him a crown that reads "serial killer", he'd take it. And he'd wear it out in public. They don't see him as a risk because he's threatened no one inside, never even said boo.'

'Is he in solitary?' Heidi asked.

'Not strict; he still gets to exercise with the others. His meals are hand delivered, though. The governor doesn't seem to know what to make of him.'

'Just covering his ass,' Bodie said.

'That sounds like our governor. Anyway, just follow old Hopkins there? He'll show you the way.'

Bodie nodded. The room went quiet. It was more than surreal, he thought, standing in such a large place, at the centre of such a mass of corrupt humanity, and to be surrounded by silence. It made the hairs stand up on the nape of his neck.

When he turned around, he saw similar disquieted feelings on the faces of his colleagues. 'You ready?' he asked.

'Not really.'

'Nope.'

'You go first, Guy.'

That last one was Heidi. Bodie looked closely at her, aware that they hadn't been able to take their relationship any further. They'd had a date night, they'd held hands. Where the hell did they go from here?

He smiled at his own reticence. This wasn't high school, and he wasn't a teenager anymore. He'd had relationships and Heidi had been married. She had a daughter. They were both people of the world, experienced, educated, proficient. Why couldn't they make the next move?

'What the hell are you smiling about?' Heidi asked.

This certainly wasn't the time or place to tell her. Everything was on hold until they got Cassidy back and dealt with LaRoy.

The older guy named Hopkins led the way. Hopkins had a stoop and walked with a slight limp, yet led them unerringly through a series of gates deeper and deeper into the heart of the prison. At first it was just offices and guard's rooms and a small café, but soon they were seeing the rows of prison cells ahead and wondering how far they had to go.

A deep silence held sway over the prison. Their footfalls sounded loud, ringing through the spaces. The lights were muted, soft in the hallways. Bodie imagined the atrocities that had been committed by the people confined to their cells, imagined the terrible, depraved images and memories that floated in the air of this place. The collected horror. If any place could project fear and revulsion and terror, if it could soak those emotions in, then it was a prison, replete with all its genuine dread. Prison was steeped in the horrible realities and fantasies of thousands of reprehensible inmates, percolating with repulsion. It hung in the air, crawled among the shadows, infested every brick and block and glass window. There was worse going on in the heads of many of these men than had been physically done, dreams and fictions that the worst of the worst wished they'd committed a thousand times.

Bodie felt like he was walking through a miasma of evil. The solitude of the night pressed in hard.

They threaded the passages, then walked through vast spaces with cells to both sides. Men's faces pressed to some doors, expressions twisted, and they whispered things, things that couldn't be heard or understood. Maybe they were chants to some unknown dark master, maybe they were promises of death. Bodie didn't know, didn't want to know. He just wished old Hopkins would pick up the pace a bit.

'Can you feel it?' Lucie whispered.

No one felt the need to ask her what she meant.

Hopkins led the way along another prison wing and then took them through another locked door. By now, the wings had turned into passageways and all the doors were locked. There weren't even peepholes.

Hopkins suddenly stopped so quickly Bodie almost bumped into him. He pointed at a door to his right.

'Antonio LaRoy lives in there,' he said.

Bodie took a long, deep breath, steeling himself, and then turned to the others.

'I hope you're ready for this,' he said.

CHAPTER TEN

The serial killer sat at the far end of a whitewashed room, perched on the edge of his bed. He sat cross-legged, with his hands resting on his knees. His body seemed oddly elongated, as if his limbs were unnaturally long – long arms, long legs, long fingers. His nose was blunt, his eyes as black as the dark heart of a madman. He was closely shaven, and when they all walked into the room, he regarded them closely.

'It is not safe for you in here,' he said immediately.

Bodie took in the cell, the washbasin and toilet, the bare walls where most men might have taped up cuttings and pictures. In this situation, he thought, Cassidy would have taken charge, immediately challenging the prisoner until he backed down. The thought made him feel both sad and angry.

'Antonio LaRoy,' he said, a statement.

'That's me,' the voice was dry, whispery.

'We need to talk to you.'

'I can see that. Fresh meat for the grinder.'

Bodie knew instinctively that Antonio was trying to unsettle them. The trouble was, it was working. Jemma and Lucie were standing with their back to the door, as far away from Antonio as they could get. Yasmine and Reilly were standing beside each other, faces white, saying nothing. Bodie and Heidi were the nearest to Antonio.

Gathering himself, he took another step forward.

'It is a good time of night to conduct a conversation,' Antonio LaRoy told them, wriggling his long fingers in Bodie's direction. 'While the masses sleep, the prison goes cold and inviting. The long-dead beasts come out.'

Bodie saw the glimmer of a smile cross Antonio's features. He tried to keep it light-hearted. 'Hey, you're my first serial killer.'

'How would you know that?'

'To my knowledge,' Bodie continued. 'I wonder how many killers normal people brush up against in their lives?'

'They are all around you,' Antonio said.

Bodie thought of the supermax. 'I'll give you that one.'

'Oh, I don't mean the prisoners.'

Bodie paused. He'd heard something, a sound, a *scraping*, outside the door. Was it the guard? But why? What would he be doing to make such a sound? It came again, the sound of furniture being dragged across a polished floor. Bodie looked at the door handle. If it were to start moving...

Antonio was still smiling faintly. 'I am not alone,' he said. 'I have my friends in here.'

Bodie was unnerved. The air was thick, cloying, as if something had drawn all the freshness out of it. He was sweating.

'Mr LaRoy,' he said. 'We have special dispensation to talk with you-'

'Do you know what I did?' Antonio interrupted.

Bodie hesitated, wondering what to say. Jemma stepped forward. 'We know all about you,' she said hoarsely.

'Oh, I doubt that. They think I killed eight. *Eight*.

Such a weak, insignificant number. They never found the rest.'

Bodie swallowed, reminded that Antonio had also told them *they never found the heads*. He really didn't want to get into that right now.

'That's not why we're here.'

'You want something from me. Something only I can give. Why else would you come in the dead of night, walking among killers, bringing your troubles to my door?'

That scraping noise came again, as if punctuating Antonio's words. Bodie wondered if he should check outside, if the door was locked, if leaving the room would gratify Antonio even more.

'What the hell is that?' Reilly said.

Bodie felt the closeness of the room, the sickening authority of the darkness that infiltrated the prison, the heavy silence.

'Do you feel their presence?' Antonio asked. 'This is the best time of the day for me. Surrounded by killers, one and all. They come to me. They congregate. We share stories.'

Bodie knew it was the circumstances, but had to admit Antonio's words were getting to him. 'You should listen to us,' he said.

'I would rather listen to *them*.'

'To the ghosts of the prison?'

'To my friends.'

Bodie watched as the man uncurled himself from the bed and rose to his feet. It was unnerving. He fought to remain in place, because his legs wanted to take a step back. Antonio's arms, in particular, were ridiculously long, as if they'd been stretched on the rack.

Antonio took a step towards them. Bodie wondered

if, before they came in here, the guy should have been restrained.

Come to think of it, where the hell was the guard? How were they supposed to find their way out of here?

Bodie felt his hair ruffled as if by a gust of wind. He grated his teeth together. Clearly, he was imagining it. Antonio had definitely got to him.

'Do you want to know what I did to them?' Antonio grinned.

'I really don't.'

'First, I stalked them. Followed them around their cities, their jobs. I learned their routines to better determine the right time to strike. You see, I already had their graves dug. It felt good, walking in their footsteps and knowing that I already knew where they were going to spend the rest of their days, rotting. Then, I started a countdown. I gave them a few days to live. I watched and waited, saw them laugh and smile with no knowledge of what was coming. I clung to the shadows, loving it. And then, when the time came-'

'We don't need to hear anymore,' Heidi said. 'We know all about your crimes.'

'But it was so beautiful,' Antonio LaRoy said. 'My only regret is that I am here, unable to repeat it again and again. Why can there not be a world for serial killers, where we play out our every fantasy, day after day, night after night, on the innocent? Oh, why?'

Bodie regarded him. The guy was quite insane, as their LaRoy had said. At the moment, he was intensely animated, his long fingers curling and waving, his arms slashing at the air as if they held a cleaver. The man was in his element.

'I drugged them, bundled them into a van, bound them top and bottom and gave them no room to move.

I drove whilst they were asleep but most of them woke before I arrived at their graves, so I talked to them, told them exactly what was about to happen, that they'd never go back to their lives, that their flesh was mine now, their blood just liquid for me to bathe in. I explained what would happen to them and where they would end up buried. That I would take their heads for my sport...' Antonio stopped there, as if worried he might reveal too much.

'Their heads?' Lucie repeated, aghast.

'Dead eyes are wonderful, did you know? They don't blink. They hold the very last image a person sees before they die? They're quite expressive. You can stare into dead eyes for hours and learn the secrets of your own existence.'

'And that's what you did?' Heidi asked.

'Of course. I planted their heads on stakes. We spoke. We stared. Dead eyes tell the story of a person's last moments, their dreams, their pain, their hopes.'

'Did you take the eyes too?' Reilly suddenly asked.

Antonio stared at him, licking his lips. 'Did I take the dead eyes from the dead heads? Did I eat them? Now that would be telling.'

'We're not here for any of that,' Bodie said.

'Oh, but I want to talk about it. As you can imagine, I don't get much chance around here.'

'We have a certain, specific set of questions to ask you,' Heidi said. 'Will you answer them?'

'I might. If you let me talk.'

So Bodie found himself regaled by tales of horrific murder and mayhem, of blood and flesh and body fluids. He already knew the rough details, but now he got the specifics. He tried to close his mind to it, tried to block it all out, but the terrible specifics kept coming.

Antonio LaRoy strode from side to side, gesticulating wildly, talking all the time, revealing already known facts with gusto and lasciviousness. He wouldn't stop. The only way they could have stopped him was to leave the room, and even then Bodie fancied the guy would just rant on.

'You're telling us nothing new,' he said at one point.

Antonio turned a shrewd eye on him. 'Oh, that's for when I really need it.'

They let him talk. An hour passed. Now they were really in the deep heart of the night. The only sound was the timbre of Antonio's voice.

Finally, he took a deep breath, turned, sat primly back down on his bed and looked up at them.

'Now,' he said. 'Tell me what you want.'

CHAPTER ELEVEN

The pure, vicious killer stalked the prison, looking for the cell of Antonio LaRoy.

In certain circles, Raffaele was famous, a consummate killer, the best of the best. They rated him as highly as Jack the Ripper, as Cassadaga, as the Jackal, if not higher. A legend come true.

First, he'd gained access to the prison using the same special dispensation as Guy Bodie and his band of relic hunters. That was clever. Mr LaRoy would never know that someone close to him had added Raffaele's name and likeness to the list.

But that only got him inside the place.

They had searched Raffaele, sent him through metal detectors, but nothing could detect the special fillet knife he carried with him everywhere. It was his trademark tool, a specially made carbon fibre instrument that fit snugly inside his long coat jacket in its comfortable, leather sheath. Raffaele had made many kills with it, and even occasionally, it had helped save his life.

Now, he stalked the prison hallways, the guard close by. Raffaele was trying to get rid of the guy, but he was sticking doggedly to his side. Raffaele knew very well that the guard thought he was part of Bodie's team, arrived late, and that he would have to do something between here and the cell to alleviate that misconception.

'I can take it from here,' he tried the most obvious route.

'You know your way?' the guard was old, rotund and slow.

'I can follow directions quite well.'

'Don't worry. I can show you so long as my old knees hold up.'

'I wouldn't want to risk that. Just tell me.'

Raffaele knew he was going to have to come up with something different. He also knew he couldn't let the guard get too close to Antonio's cell.

'Is there a restroom?' he asked.

The old guard turned to look at him, footsteps echoing in the silent halls. 'You got a weak bladder?'

Raffaele tucked his curly blonde hair behind both ears. 'It's been a while.'

The guard sighed, then waved at an alcove. 'You can go in there. Make it quick. I don't have all friggin' night.'

Raffaele thought that's exactly what the guard *did* have. What else was he going to do on his long night shift? The fat old bastard probably wanted to get back to his plastic desk and his plastic chair and his nightly rerun of Battlestar Galactica.

But he needed to get the old bastard closer.

'This one?' he paused and then walked slowly, as if nervous.

The guard sighed and pushed past him, leading the way. Excellent.

Raffaele fell in behind him. He looked to the walls, saw the angle of the nearest camera. The lazy guard probably wouldn't be watching anyway, but Raffaele never took a chance.

The guard pushed on the door of the restroom, holding it open for him.

'You're on your own from here,' the old man said with a smug grin.

Raffaele now felt quite good about introducing him to the fillet knife. Normally, he killed to order, but stuck only to the specific target. Collateral damage was not entertained, nor needed. Tonight, however, his boss had been quite detailed.

Do anything you have to. No messing about. Just get through this and give me the information I need.

Raffaele walked past the guard, grabbed his shirt collar, and then hauled him into the toilet with a tug of insane strength. The guard flew forward, almost hauled off his feet, staggering until he face-planted the floor.

Raffaele stood over him.

'I think I'd like you to accompany me,' he said.

From the folds of his coat, he produced the wicked-looking fillet knife. The guard's eyes locked onto it and grew wide. Raffaele wasn't one to prolong his kills – he wasn't one of those who enjoyed his victim's fear or death throes – so he plunged the knife into the back of the guard's neck and slit lengthways before jumping away from the flow of blood. The guard died in silence, in shock, never knowing what was really happening.

Raffaele stood over the leaking body.

He would be okay. There would be no patrols, no seeking of this guard until he didn't return to his post. He already knew exactly where Antonio's cell room was, and knew it wouldn't take him long to get there. He also knew the positions of the cameras and believed he could avoid being seen. That was if the lazy guards were even watching, which they probably weren't.

Raffaele smelled the fresh blood of his latest kill. It made his nostrils flair. This was the right place for death. The air practically reeked of it. Or, more precisely, of the *fantasy* of it. Raffaele wiped the fillet knife off and replaced it into its sheath, and then his jacket. He pulled the old guard further into the toilet, taking care not to get blood on his shoes. Next, he opened the toilet door and walked nonchalantly out, making sure he avoided the nearest camera, now hugging the wall, all pretence of being the innocent visitor gone.

Raffaele was from a long line of killers. Some of his ancestors had even been executed by kings and queens. Quite the claim to fame. The tainted bloodline – if that's what it was – ran through his lineage for centuries, each generation producing a killer. Raffaele had grown up in the easiest of circumstances, with a wealthy family, caring parents, staff on hand to cater to his every whim. He had every chance to turn out right. But somehow... something had whittled its way inside him, something obscene and evil. Raffaele had been haunted since his early years; he knew he was different.

The first incident came at age ten, when he had *accidentally* pushed the waiter down the stairs. He had laughed inside to see the man flying clumsily downstairs, bouncing from step to step, the drinks on his tray spraying everywhere, his limbs splayed. The sound of breaking bones had been a particular delight to Raffaele's ears.

The waiter survived. He blamed Raffaele. All this did was instil in the young killer a sense of caution. Next time, he'd have to cover his tracks better. The event was put down to an accident. Raffaele got past it. The waiter didn't. He never recovered. Later, he was fired. By that time, Raffaele was planning his next attack.

He didn't bother with animals. They weren't challenging enough for him. He grew in age and stature, and put bodies in the ground. Later, Raffaele admitted to it all in some kind of confidential newspaper article where he'd been interviewed behind closed doors. *The Italian Press Meets the Serial Killer.* Something like that.

Raffaele didn't see himself as a serial killer.

He was a paid hitman, and he liked that. It gave him leave to murder a particular target and then move on. There was always someone else who needed killing. Raffaele found his occupation to be more than a full-time job. If you wanted to, you could kill twenty-four hours a day, seven days a week and still not see an end to your victims.

Raffaele liked that.

He moved on now, trying not to reflect on his raft of victims. In his mind, every single one lived, from the very first to the old guard. He thought it ironic that the men and women he killed lived on in his own mind. He'd seen their death throes, heard their last breaths, experienced how they handled the swift onslaught of death. That moment... when they knew they were going to die. Raffaele enjoyed revisiting those moments, letting the dead live in his mind's eye, seeing the blood surge out of their bodies.

The prison hunkered dark and silent all around him. Raffaele had been sent to persuade Antonio to give up his line of stanza. He had been sent not by LaRoy, the big boss, but by Friday, his second in command. Now Friday was offering big numbers in the way of bucks, privilege in the way of being chosen for the most delicious future kills. LaRoy didn't know about Friday's betrayal, but Friday wanted those lines of stanza desperately. Something about a pile of gemstones, some damn treasure at the end of the rainbow.

Raffaele cared little for treasure. He did like what Friday was offering, though. Friday thought he could control LaRoy's dubious business empire from the inside by keeping LaRoy as the figurehead and just pulling his strings. At least, that was Friday's plan. It didn't matter to Raffaele who was in charge, as long as he got the work.

Raffaele moved through the darkness. He crept along a narrow passage, took the darker branch deeper into the prison. There was an unnatural hush all around him, broken by the screams of prisoners as they woke from terrible dreams, by the rubberised boots of guards, by the hum and clank of the forced air system.

The shadows embraced him. He came so close to a guard that he could have sliced off an ear, and the man never even knew he was there, never sensed the terrible hulking presence of death at his back. The guard was lucky Raffaele had but one job to do.

Antonio.

Raffaele paused. Antonio's cell was ahead.

CHAPTER TWELVE

Bodie looked closely at Antonio. *Tell me what you want.* Was this madman really going to help them?

'We know about your father,' Jemma ventured. 'What he did to all of you. The mind games. The abuse. The way he treated you.'

'My father,' Antonio said. 'Was the worst of all of us. *He* should have been locked away. The keys melted. The location forgotten. Nothing he did to us was right.'

'All seven of you.' Heidi said.

Her words gave the serial killer pause. He stopped and looked at her, his eyes reflective. 'Yes,' he said. 'Seven brothers and sisters.'

'Do you ever wonder what they're doing now?' Lucie asked.

Antonio blinked rapidly and then shook his head, as if the question caused him pain. Perhaps it did, bringing with it memories of childhood. The thought of siblings also raised the question of mortality.

'I don't like that question,' he said. 'Why am I here?'

'Like I said, we need your help,' Bodie said. 'Your father-'

'Stop talking about my father!'

Bodie backed off. Antonio's muscles were bunched, his fists clenched. He regarded them through eyes that blazed with hatred.

Bodie held out a hand. 'All right. How about your brother, LaRoy? Can I talk about him?'

'Which one?'

Bodie was suddenly aware they'd never caught LaRoy's first name and didn't know that much about the man who'd kidnapped Cassidy. Again, he changed tack.

'The family wealth,' he said. 'It's dwindling. We know about the gemstones.'

'The gemstones?' Antonio looked blank.

'They were hidden when you were young,' Bodie carefully didn't mention the father. 'Do you remember?' All he needed now was for Antonio's addled mind to fail to bring up the memory.

But after a moment, Antonio's face changed. He looked at Bodie with a shrewd eye. 'You're looking for the gemstones?'

'Your brother is. We've been brought in to help.'

Bodie watched the play of emotions across the man's face. He took a second to look around, saw the anxious looks on the faces of his team, drank in the overwhelming silence. In here, they might as well be in solitary confinement. He couldn't remember ever feeling so isolated.

The doorknob turned.

Bodie's heart slammed into his throat. In here, standing before a killer, surrounded by a silence worse than death, Bodie was watching the slow, deliberate turning of the doorknob. The guard shouldn't be out there. They had a radio to contact him.

So who the hell was turning...

Bodie saw the movement end, the knob twist back into place. Of course, the door was locked. That was protocol. Could a prisoner have got out?

Bodie nodded at the doorknob and his team glanced over questioningly.

'It just turned,' he said.

They frowned. They looked back at him. 'Are you sure?'

Was he? Even now, the moment felt ridiculous. Maybe his imagination was playing tricks on him. Maybe being in this place had upset his normally robust mind.

He stared. The doorknob didn't move again. Bodie took a tentative glance back at Antonio.

The serial killer was watching him, a slight smile on his face. 'It definitely moved,' he said.

And now Bodie wondered if the man was teasing him, playing him, trying to get even further inside his head. These mind games were horrific.

'We are not alone,' Antonio said.

Bodie glared at him. They couldn't let this guy get the upper hand. 'Stop with the bullshit,' he said, ignoring the doorknob incident for now. They'd deal with that when they needed to leave the cell.

Antonio held up a long-fingered hand. 'I haven't lied to you yet, have I? There is something dark abroad in the prison tonight.'

'What do you mean?' Lucie asked.

'A different presence. As I'm sure you know, when you live somewhere, constantly, you gain an affinity with it. You come to know the sounds, the whispers, the general atmosphere, the way the very air breathes. Well, tonight it is wrong.'

'Wrong?' Yasmine echoed.

'Something else walks among us. I can smell fresh blood in the air.'

Bodie had had enough. He knew Antonio would want to scare them, might even want to prolong the interview for his own gratification. He sought to steer the conversation back to the point.

'The gemstones,' he said. 'You remember them then?'

'Oh, yes. Good old daddy dear secreted millions of dollars' worth of precious diamonds and rubies and more away, knowing that, one day, one of us would need them.'

So now he seemed to have no problem mentioning his father. Bodie sighed.

'Can you tell us your line of the stanza?'

Antonio blinked at them. 'You're just asking? You're not going to try to force it out of me?' he seemed disappointed.

Bodie heard a noise at his back, turned swiftly to take another look at the doorknob, but it was just Reilly making himself more comfortable. Bodie sighed.

Antonio regarded him slyly. 'You're in my world now.'

'How about that line of stanza?' Heidi said.

'I could give it to you. My father beat it into us, made us remember each line succinctly. How many do you have so far?'

'One,' Reilly said before anyone could stop him.

'One? Is that all? I am the first person you would visit after my brother?'

'Or maybe you were the closest.'

'Closest? Then you have come from New York where my brother, Manny, holds sway over the family fortunes.'

Bodie was glad to get a first name for the tyrant who had Cass. He wasn't sure how it would help them yet.

'What was his line of the stanza?' Antonio asked, seemingly quite lucid now.

'Line one,' Reilly said. 'A ghost town famous in the nineteenth century.'

Antonio pursed his lips at that, as Bodie gave Reilly a warning look. The guy was new to the team. He didn't know to play his cards close to his chest. Not yet. Bodie would have to apprise him.

'And your line?' Heidi prompted.

Antonio cleared his throat. 'Do you know why my father gave us the seven lines?' he asked.

Bodie's reply, *'cos you're all fucking crazy,'* didn't cross his lips. A silence stretched.

'It fed our loss of control, messed with our sense of right and wrong. My father was a master manipulator. The very best. He set out to turn his seven kids into addle-brained idiots, maybe even killers. Well, he succeeded.'

'You're saying he started you off on your journey to be a serial killer, to murder eight people?' Lucie asked with surprise in her voice.

'Eight?' Antonio repeated with a malicious grin. 'No, not *eight*. It's the same old question: nurture or nature. Well, he nurtured us into losing our minds.'

Bodie was at a loss, unsure how to approach the man. He was chatty, deadly, obviously out of his mind. He moved around with an economy of movement and seemed to enjoy trying to shock them. Bodie was highly conscious of the vast, lethal prison all around them. The locked door, the doorknob that he was sure had turned. In here, all was silent. The sense of isolation was intense. For Bodie, though, it just served to highlight the horrific vastness that surrounded them.

'Why are you working for Manny?' Antonio asked shrewdly.

Bodie gave Reilly a quick warning glance before the man blurted anything out. He thought about an answer. In the end, though, what did it matter?

'He took a friend of ours,' he said. 'We're being forced to do this.'

Antonio raised an eyebrow at that. 'What is your friend's name?'

'Cassidy,' Again, how could it hurt?

'Cassidy,' Antonio rolled the name around his mouth, his tongue darting back and forth. It was a strange sound and Bodie instantly regretted giving Antonio the name.

'It feels good in my mouth.' Antonio clenched his teeth at them.

Bodie feared they were losing him once more to madness.

'Please,' he said. 'The line?'

And then Antonio threw himself at them.

CHAPTER THIRTEEN

Bodie flung up a hand, tried to ward the man off. The figure hit him hard, knocking him to his knees, and Bodie heard the teeth gnashing inches from his flesh. He pushed out with his other hand, felt Antonio's hard body, tried to ward the man off.

Reilly was already there, grabbing Antonio around the throat and hauling him off. Bodie was suddenly struck by the contrast between Reilly and Cassidy. On any normal day, it would be Cassidy fighting, Cassidy dragging the attacker away. But with Cassidy absent, it was Reilly who stepped up.

Antonio suddenly burst out laughing, cackling. He doubled over in Reilly's arms, laughing until the tears fell from his eyes.

'Oh, that was good. So good. Are you going to blab to the guards?'

Bodie stood up, dusted himself off. Antonio was hanging in Reilly's grip, stomach heaving with mirth.

'Did I bite you?'

Bodie took a long, deep breath. Damn, this was unsettling. If it wasn't for Cassidy, he'd be hauling his ass right out of this godforsaken hole and never looking back.

'The line of the stanza,' he said. 'Please.'

'What's in it for me?'

Bodie hesitated. Now this was real talk he could deal

with. He motioned to Reilly to let go of Antonio. The serial killer stayed on his knees, looking up as Reilly backed away.

'What do you want?' Heidi asked.

Bodie waited. He already knew that Manny LaRoy held enormous sway in this prison. He had helped elect its governor. They had been authorised to give Antonio almost anything he might want.

'Flesh,' Antonio said breathlessly. 'Eyes that I might fry with asparagus and a hint of blood-infused sauce, washed down with a fruity merlot.'

'Books,' Bodie said frostily. 'Money. Extra sessions in the sun. Daily papers. Better food. Take your pick.'

'I want it all.'

'I thought you might. I can do that. Give us the line.'

Antonio opened his mouth to speak.

Outside the door, Raffaele could hear everything. He was crouched in a narrow passage with shadows pressed all around. It was so dark he couldn't see the ceiling, so quiet he could hear the steady beat of his own heart. He'd already checked the door, made sure that it was locked. That fact put him in a more difficult position. He knew there were five people in there with Antonio, but would have fancied his chances against them. The violence would have helped persuade Antonio to talk. Maybe he could even have offered the dead bodies to the serial killer, maybe the eyes.

Raffaele, listening, liked the way Antonio thought.

Visions of violence swam in his own head. Raffaele fought hard to quell them. Right here, right now, wasn't the place to indulge them.

He was a consummate professional. He needed to

act like one. The only distraction was Antonio's words, his total embrace of the bloodiest of lifestyles. It called to Raffaele. It moved him. He...

A noise snapped him instantly back to the present. The long corridor he was in let out into one of the main halls, where cells lined both sides. Just then, the door at the end of the corridor had opened.

A guard was framed in the entryway.

Raffaele crouched further down, blending with the darkness. He was but a shadow, unmoving, silent as the guard crept forward. Even from here, he could tell the guard didn't want to be here.

But the man walked down the corridor. As he moved further, sets of lights illuminated in the ceiling, marking his steps. The lights were automatic and, when they reached Raffaele, would light him up like a damn bonfire.

He slipped the fillet knife from his jacket.

Raffaele was caught in two minds. He wasn't sure if this guy was the guard assigned to the relic hunters or just a man on patrol. Maybe he was coming to join them, to let them out. Or maybe he was just performing a random circuit.

The guard's radio crackled. He spoke into it. Raffaele waited. The guy was now just eight doors down. Soon, the bank of lights that governed the spaces outside Antonio's door would blink into light.

And then... and then... blood.

The guard walked forward nonchalantly, oblivious.

Raffaele darted forward, knife poised. He hit the guard in the chest, driving him back. The man's eyes opened wide, he opened his mouth, but then Raffaele slit his throat from ear to ear. He saw the wound open wide, heard the gurgle in the man's throat. He jumped away, let the guy collapse to the floor amidst pouring blood.

The guard collapsed face first.

Raffaele turned back to the door, its thickness the only thing barring the killer from the throats of the relic hunters.

Bodie held up a hand sharply. Again, he thought he'd heard something. Maybe a scuffle in the corridor outside. The thud of a body hitting the floor. His heart pounded. He glanced at Antonio, knowing exactly what the man would say.

'I told you. We are not alone. The blood scent blooms.'

Bodie could smell nothing, and now he could hear nothing. Was somebody standing on the other side? Waiting? Not in this prison, surely, not even in the dead of night. How the hell would they even get in here?

'This is all to do with me,' Antonio said.

'This has nothing to do with you,' Bodie imagined the serial killer was going into narcissistic mode, a non-quality they all shared. He wanted to shake the man until he gave up the line.

'How about that offer?' Lucie prompted.

'Books. Papers. Money. A bit of freedom. What can I do with that? What can *I* do? Don't you remember – I am a man who eats flesh, who boils eyeballs, who bathes in the blood of his victims. I am the great serial killer who murdered dozens and then ate their heads. Isn't that what they say? The great serial killer who cannibalised his targets.'

'They don't say fuck all about you, bud,' Reilly said.

Bodie cringed. That wasn't the state of mind they wanted Antonio to adopt. They wanted him self-absorbed, amenable, full of himself. They wanted him talking and off-guard.

'The line?' he asked again.

'I scraped the flesh from each skull, boiled it until it sizzled. I marinated it with blood and honey and barbecue sauce. I scooped out the... *the eighteen million dollar goldmine...*' Antonio blinked and looked up at them, as surprised to hear he'd blurted out the line as they were.

Bodie frowned. 'That's it?'

'I was given line three of the stanza. It is *the eighteen million dollar goldmine.*'

Bodie almost pitied the man for his madness. And all this is due to the father. If there had ever been a man more worthy of Hell, Bodie hadn't yet come across him.

'Radio the guards,' he said.

He didn't want to stay a minute more in this hellhole than he had to.

The room was cloying, suffocating. It was filled with the presence of death, of murder and mayhem. Antonio basked in it. That was why he was so amenable. The man was in his element.

'Call the damn guards,' Bodie said.

'I *am* doing,' Heidi held up her hand with the radio clasped in it.

Antonio had fallen silent, perhaps wondering how he'd got tongue twisted and revealed his big secret. He asked them for extra books, papers, time in the sun. Bodie just nodded, eager to get away.

He walked over to the doorknob, heard Heidi talking to the guards as he twisted it. He wasn't unhappy about finding it locked. Yes, it was supposed to be locked, but you never could tell. He wished there was a vision panel that enabled him to look out into the hallway.

Minutes passed before two guards arrived, and then the shouting started.

CHAPTER FOURTEEN

It took the rest of the night, but they cleared the relic hunters of any wrongdoing. There was a camera inside Antonio's cell, and it recorded the fact that they'd never left. It even saw the moment when the doorknob had turned.

Bodie glanced at his friends. 'I knew I saw something,' he had said.

'We were that close to the killer?' Heidi said.

'He had to have heard everything,' Reilly said. 'You know that, don't you?'

'At least he was gone when the other guards arrived,' Lucie shuddered.

'It's the name on the special dispensation that worries me,' Bodie said after a while. 'Raffaele. Scanned in on *our* dispensation. How does that happen?'

'Clearly, it was added,' Reilly said. 'But by who?'

'It's all under Manny LaRoy's name,' Lucie said. 'I honestly don't understand it.'

Bodie sighed. 'It's clear there's another party involved,' he said. 'Someone working against us and LaRoy. Someone with an intimate knowledge of his business.'

Reilly nodded. 'I agree.'

They were heading away from the supermax. It was after three in the morning and a vast bank of low clouds had cloaked any light from the sky. They reached the car, jumped in and started driving away from the prison, glad to leave it in their rearview.

Within minutes Bodie had taken the burner phone out of his pocket and made a call. It was answered almost immediately.

'What time of day do you call this?' LaRoy growled.

'Shut up, asshole. Put her on the line.'

'Who?'

Bodie felt his teeth grate together as Reilly drove the car, guiding them through the night. 'Don't fuck with me.'

'Oh, I wouldn't dream of it. But Cassidy is temporarily indisposed right now.'

'We have the third line of the LaRoy stanza. I want proof of life.'

There was a sigh. 'You're going to do this with every line, aren't you?'

'I'm not an idiot.'

'Well, you lot got yourselves into this fix to begin with, so...'

'Just put Cass on the line.'

LaRoy told him to hold on. It made sense that the guy would be in bed and probably had to make his way to some cell or other. Whilst he did, Bodie told him the rest of the news.

'There was someone else in there with us tonight.'

'Well, it was a prison.'

'I mean someone after the same thing as we were. They killed guards, tried to get into the room.'

There was a long silence, and then LaRoy let out another sigh, this one deeper and more aggrieved. 'I fear there is someone in my organisation, someone close to me, who is working against me. The investigations are ongoing.'

'Whoever it was, they're good,' Bodie told him. 'They hired a guy who took out at least two guards, used our own special dispensation against us, and planned to attack us in that room. All of us. In the end, I think he overheard Antonio giving us the third line of the stanza and called it a day.'

'The rat will be rooted out.'

'Do it quick.'

'Tell me the third line of the stanza.'

'First... Cassidy.'

LaRoy said nothing. Long minutes passed. Bodie could tell from the noises coming through the phone that LaRoy was walking somewhere. Eventually, he heard LaRoy bark out an order.

'Open the door.'

Bodie gripped the phone harder.

Then LaRoy's voice. 'Oh, Cassidy. Oh, Cassidy dear. I hate to wake you, sweetheart, but I have a man on the phone. He wants to talk to you. Would that be okay?'

Bodie heard a muttering and a visceral volley of curse words. Cassidy sounded in good voice.

LaRoy's voice came back on the phone. 'That good enough for you, or do I need to chop something off?'

'I promise... if you hurt her...'

'Oh, we haven't touched a hair on her little red head. She's merchandise, pure and simple. You don't harm your merchandise.'

Bodie gave him the line and hung up the phone, let out a curse of his own. Around him, everyone was silent, no doubt all thinking the same thing about their captive friend.

Bodie glanced over at Reilly. 'Where the hell are you going?'

'I don't know,' Reilly admitted. 'We've passed the prison twice.'

'Next stop, the mental institution for what LaRoy says is the lunatic,' Jemma said. 'We have the special dispensation to get in there, too.'

'Yeah? Let's hope no one else does.'

They drove to the nearest hotel, rented rooms, and settled in for the rest of the night. The mental institution they would be visiting was also situated in upstate New York, and they could be there in just over an hour. The earliest they could get in was 11 a.m. the next day. Bodie tossed and turned on his hard hotel bed. The air con was broken, and the room was stifling. They hadn't even provided a fan. He found that staying awake was worse than trying to sleep. The heat came in waves.

By 6 a.m. he had had enough, took a cold shower and then sought breakfast. The little nook they called the breakfast bar was cooler and Bodie sat there for quite a while, picking at croissants and toasts, jam and butter, all washed down with endless amounts of coffee. Soon, the others joined him, all complaining about their airless, roasting night, but not too loudly. It was as if Cassidy's plight made their own pale into insignificance. No hardship could come close to what their friend was enduring.

They ate and drank and discussed the two lines of stanza until checkout time. Then, they climbed into the car, set the sat nav for the mental institution, and followed the road. The roads were composed of long winding bends lined by tall trees and, at first, were quiet. At one point, they ended up following a long trailer full of stripped tree trunks and took fifteen minutes to get past. They filled up at a solitary gas station, grabbing snacks and drinks and taking in the cool air, grateful for it after last night. Bodie fancied his body temperature had just about returned to normal.

They arrived at the Hampton Psychiatric Hospital a little after eleven, parked up, and made their way to the door. It was a forbidding, red brick building with a tall edifice that towered over the sloping lands below. As Bodie walked up to the doors, he felt the overbearing frontage looming above. There were hundreds of windows, all white framed and uniform, and even a tower and turret on the far side, something to break up the monotony.

Bodie pushed through the narrow front door into what might have been a living room. There were a couple of sofas, a TV on the wall showing some kind of uplifting documentary about Hampton Psychiatric Hospital, several low-slung coffee tables and flowery wallpaper on the walls. Bodie spied a desk opposite and a nurse standing behind.

He walked over, gave them their names, waited. By now, he knew what was coming. The confusion, the odd looks as the special dispensation was found, the sighing, the grudging acceptance that there was extra work to do.

'Don't worry,' Heidi told them. 'It won't take long.'

Her words didn't help. They were asked to wait until the staff could find a nurse to accompany them to Leanne LaRoy's room. At this time of day, they said, she was out in the gardens taking the air.

As he waited, Bodie went over what they knew of Leanne LaRoy from the folder. She had been incarcerated in the mental institution for a series of ever-worsening deeds. First, despite all her money, she had been caught shoplifting. Leanne had no knowledge of what she'd done, and no motive for it. Bouts of harassment followed the shoplifting, and then bodily harm to two of her boyfriends. The counts against her racked up. When she claimed loss of cognitive ability, her family stepped in. Rather than let her go to prison, they'd confined her to this psychiatric facility for close and further observation. Money talked. Leanne's victims were paid off. Charges were dropped. Leanne was quietly whisked away. Some of this information had come from LaRoy, some from Lucie's research into the woman, but Bodie wondered how the intervening years had treated her.

'They forgot about her,' Lucie told them. 'Left her rotting away in here. Gone. Forgotten. Out of sight,' she shook her head. 'This family is reprehensible.'

'They seem... eccentric,' Reilly said.

Lucie looked up at him from her perch. 'Eccentric isn't the right word, my friend. She should be receiving proper treatment. LaRoy should oversee it all.'

'We know what LaRoy is,' Bodie grated. 'He's a killer, a wealthy madman. And I have no doubt he'll kill Cassidy in an instant if we don't come through. We're all she's got, guys. Whatever it takes to save her.'

They all nodded.

Whatever it takes.

CHAPTER FIFTEEN

Bodie said, 'Heads up. The quicker we get this done, the better.'

A nurse was approaching, clad in a white gown that flowed around her body and legs. She gave them a tired smile.

'You are Leanne's visitors?'

Bodie nodded, standing. 'We are.'

'Good. I have her set up in an interview room.'

It sounded formal. Maybe that was a good thing. Bodie didn't fancy being locked in a room again, as they had been with Antonio. They followed the nurse along a white-tiled corridor and then through a couple of locked doors before emerging into a wider space that acted as a kind of chill-out area for the patients. There were round white tables and plastic chairs and a TV on the wall, at a low volume, this one showing a cartoon of some sort. Two people sat watching it.

The nurse led them through the room, past a few open doors, and then stopped outside a final, closed door. This one looked much more official, with bars over the vision panel and a chunky lock. The nurse tapped at the door.

'Leanne,' she said in a bright voice. 'I have your visitors.'

Bodie followed the nurse into the room, his friends at his side. The nurse turned and took a swift look at them.

'Do you all have to be in here?'

Bodie understood the comment. He turned to the others. 'Reilly, Yasmine, Heidi. Why don't you wait outside?'

He wanted the two women he considered the most relatable to stay with him. Out of the three of them, only Heidi raised her eyebrows in question.

The nurse wasn't done. 'Speak carefully and succinctly. Ask your questions in a civil manner. Be aware, Leanne has a reputation for violence. Do not antagonise her. You are here at our own risk and have waived all rights. Do you understand?'

Bodie didn't. He hadn't known that, but they still had no choice. He nodded and watched the nurse leave the room, and then turned his full attention to Leanne.

The woman had short-cropped silver hair and a prematurely lined face. Her dark blue eyes bulged. She regarded them without expression and sat without moving a single muscle. She wore a white blouse and blue jeans and was clad in hospital slippers. Her hands rested on the white tabletop, fingers splayed, and she breathed easily through her open mouth. Bodie regarded her carefully.

'Leanne,' he said. 'I am Guy Bodie. I know your brother, Manny LaRoy.'

He winced inwardly, knowing he had no choice but to mention her brother.

'Do you remember him?'

The white face gazed back at him impassively, as if set in stone.

'They have asked me to come visit, to offer you anything you want.' It had worked with Antonio. Maybe it would work with Leanne.

The eyes didn't flicker. The body barely moved as the woman breathed slowly.

Jemma stepped forward. 'Please,' she said. 'You could help us out.'

Bodie toyed with the idea of revealing all to Leanne, then decided not to. There was an odd atmosphere in the room, one of suppressed violence. He watched the hands, the arms, the legs. If Leanne coiled or reared back or raised a hand in anger, he was ready to act.

The woman watched them with bulging eyes.

'I genuinely want to help you,' he said. 'Make your stay here more comfortable. How can we do that?'

Nothing. The woman didn't even twitch.

Bodie kept a close eye on her limbs, waiting for some kind of explosion. He knew that Reilly, Yasmine and Heidi were stationed just outside the door, and also kept an ear open in that direction. Whoever was stalking their movements, looking for the same lines of stanza, wouldn't be too far away.

It was time to probe deeper.

'Leanne,' he kept it personal. 'We need your help. Your father gave you a line of the LaRoy stanza many years ago. He made you remember it. We need to know that line.'

There it was, laid out in simple terms. Was there a flicker in Leanne's eyes? A touch of recognition?

'Please,' Jemma came forward again. 'We need your help. It's imperative we have that line.'

Leanne finally cracked her face. She frowned and turned to stare at Jemma.

'Fuck off,' she said.

Bodie had been hoping for a miracle. It clearly wasn't going to happen. This woman had been basically locked away in a psychiatric hospital for something approaching ten years. No one visited her, no one except the staff cared for her. This was just as bad as solitary confinement, but with a few bells on. Leanne had gone back to her thousand-yard stare, her face expressionless.

Bodie believed they didn't have a lot of time. The killer, Raffaele, wouldn't be far away. He gave Jemma a long look and then nodded.

Jemma stepped forward, held her hands out. 'Your brother has our friend. Her name is Cassidy. She's a good person. She's helped lots of people. Your brother has threatened to kill her if we don't get the line of the stanza from you.'

Now Leanne shifted her head a little so that she could gaze right into Jemma's eyes. Her mouth opened. Her eyelids twitched. She answered Jemma's heartfelt appeal with two single words.

'Fuck. Off,' she said.

CHAPTER SIXTEEN

This time, Raffaele had brought two other guys with him. He wasn't happy about it. LaRoy's second-in-command, Friday, had insisted on it. The guy's names were Carpenter and Cheng. For some reason, Friday wasn't happy with the last outing.

'We won,' Raffaele had said. 'I got the line.'

'I don't see it that way,' Friday had whispered back.

'Why are you whispering?'

'Because I'm in a goddamn house surrounded by dozens of potential snitches and watched by a boss who has to be the most paranoid bastard I've ever known. Running this operation is as hard as it gets.'

Raffaele didn't pity his boss. Friday had brought all this hardship down on himself by betraying the big boss, Manny LaRoy. If he didn't pay so well, Raffaele would be firmly on the other side.

'In any case,' Friday had told him. 'The men are there to help you, to make things go more smoothly. You can't repeat what happened at the prison. LaRoy already suspects everyone. This time, I need you to get in and get out. Efficient, silent, flow in and out like a placid river. You get me?'

Raffaele said that he did, and he accepted the men because he had no choice. That still didn't mean he was going to do this Friday's way.

He didn't do placid.

It was just gone one in the afternoon. Raffaele had parked on the road outside the facility, watching and waiting. So far, he'd seen no sign of the so-called relic hunters, no external security other than a few cameras, and no comings and goings. The facility really was tight. He still had the same special dispensation Guy Bodie and co. had, but this time Raffaele didn't want to risk that. The relic hunters would be wise to it now. He wondered where they were. Perhaps they'd come and gone.

The car was silent. Both Carpenter and Cheng didn't talk much, which suited Raffaele just fine. He sat there and watched... and watched... waiting for something.

It came a little after 8 p.m.

Darkness fell. That was what Raffaele wanted. The facility's lights went on, the parking area illuminated by just one lamp, the exterior brickwork lit up by only three. Raffaele saw several members of staff leave the place, saw the night watch come in. He told the men in the back seat what they were going to do.

'Isn't that the exact opposite of what Friday wants?' Carpenter asked.

'I'm calling the shots in the field. This is the best course of action.'

They waited. Darkness claimed the land completely. They cracked open their doors, drew their weapons, guns, and knives, and hurried up the slope that led to the front door. Raffaele entered first and approached the nurse at the desk.

'I'm sorry-' she began.

'So am I,' Raffaele said, and shot her in the face.

It was a suppressed weapon, so the gunshots sounded like two sudden pops. The nurse flew backwards amidst a welter of blood. Raffaele strode quickly around the desk, looked at a row of CCTV monitors and several buttons. He pressed the one that read: *Internal Doors*.

There was a click. Carpenter rushed over to the door and held it open. Together, the three of them dashed through, ran up a white-tiled corridor and came to another door. This one was also open. Eventually, the corridor opened out into a wide common room full of plastic tables and chairs.

Raffaele moved unerringly toward his source.

He knew the layout, knew where Leanne's room was, even knew the positions of the guards and their own rooms. He paused to the left of an open door, took a quick look inside.

Two guards were sitting back, enjoying drinks and bags of fries, their paunches rolling over their belts, their laughter filling the room. They were lazy, incompetent, in Raffaele's eyes, and they didn't deserve to live.

He could have bypassed them. Instead, he crept into the room, came up behind them, and put a bullet in each of their brain pans. The men fell forward, instantly dead as their blood coated the walls.

Carpenter and Cheng watched soundlessly. Raffaele knew they were already scared of him. This kind of behaviour would cow them even further. Good.

He exited the room and moved on. Two doors down, three. It all looked the same. There were vision panels in the doors, but he didn't use any of them. His attention was affixed on just one place.

Leanne LaRoy's room.

It wasn't far. Raffaele stopped right outside it, tried it. Obviously, it was locked. Raffaele didn't worry. He stepped back, aimed the gun and without a word shot off the lock and the door handle. The bullet pinged away, narrowly missing Carpenter. Raffaele shrugged. He didn't care.

Inside, a woman with silver hair and buggy eyes was just coming awake. She sat up in bed, blinking; her gaze already fixed on Raffaele. The killer didn't hesitate. He ran straight at her, giving her no time to think. Even so, she batted at him with powerful arms, catching him around the head and the ears. Raffaele caught her wrists and clasped them tightly.

'If I have to hurt you, I will,' he said. 'Stop hitting me.'

The woman responded by pulling a crazed face and redoubling her efforts. Raffaele knew he couldn't kill her, couldn't hurt her too badly. They needed the information that she could give. He held on and then elbowed her in the nose.

Blood spurted.

Raffaele bent one of her wrists at a dangerous angle so that it was close to breaking. 'Desist,' he said.

Leanne spat at him, but then went still. Now, she was staring at the far wall, her eyes fixed so intently that Raffaele turned to look at what she was seeing. But it was just a white wall.

'What the fuck's the witch looking at?' Carpenter grumbled.

Raffaele waved his gun at the man. 'Shut up,' he said.

He turned back to Leanne. 'Answer my question,' he said. 'And I won't hurt you. I will leave you here. Now tell me, what is your line of the LaRoy stanza?'

Leanne's eyes flickered. Maybe it was in recognition of being asked the same thing earlier that day, Raffaele thought. He was sure Bodie and his cronies would already have been here. He wondered what Leanne had told them.

The woman didn't look at him. She stared at the wall as if fixated on an all-important snippet of news.

Raffaele clubbed her across the temple with the butt of his gun. 'Tell me.'

She spat on her covers.

This wasn't working. Raffaele considered who they working with, what her plight might be. In his experience, everyone responded to pain. It was the common denominator. Maybe it was time for the knife.

'I will hurt you badly,' he said.

And then she turned to him so swiftly it made him flinch. Her big eyes were on him, her tongue flicking between her lips.

'I welcome it,' she said.

Raffaele hit her with the gun again.

She smiled. Licked her lips. She offered the side of her head to the butt of his gun.

'Again,' she said.

Raffaele realised this still wasn't working. Maybe permanent disfigurement would stand a better chance.

He pocketed the gun, let her see the knife, turned it left and right before her eyes. The woman just licked her lips.

'Do it,' she said.

Raffaele called her bluff. He dug the point of the knife into her cheek, dug it in so that the blood welled up, and then cut straight down, ending at her chin. Leanne didn't flinch. She stuck out her tongue to catch the blood.

'It makes me feel... alive,' she said.

Raffaele dug the knife in again, gave her matching tramlines. The blood was dripping to the floor in a constant flow now, pooling. The woman turned her head so that she could look straight at Raffaele.

'Don't stop,' she told him.

Damn it, this wasn't working too. Raffaele had known nothing like it. Usually, at this point, he would just kill the mark and move on. But he couldn't kill this woman. He needed the information that she held in that decayed brain.

What to do?

He glanced back at Carpenter and Cheng. They were standing with their mouths hanging open, shock on their faces. They were no good at all. Their guns and knives were held limply in both hands.

Raffaele wondered if a good stabbing in the stomach would help.

And then he decided *no*. It wouldn't. He was very conscious of the passage of time. So far, they'd been lucky. The woman at the front desk and the guards hadn't been found. That luck wouldn't hold.

It was running out even now.

Raffaele wondered as to his options. He needed time to work on her. At the moment, she was loving it. Give him an hour or two and she'd be in bloody ribbons. He'd be working on her guts, worse. He wanted that, knew it was the only thing that would get him what he wanted.

'Grab her,' he said.

Both Carpenter and Cheng looked at him with shocked looks on their faces. 'What?'

'Grab the bitch's arms and legs. We're taking her with us.'

Several things happened at once. Carpenter and Cheng hastily pocketed their weapons. Raffaele walked forward to supervise, but Leanne gave them an open-mouthed, horror-stricken look.

'*No,*' she said.

Raffaele ignored her, watched as Carpenter and Cheng closed in.

Leanne went crazy, punching and kicking and screaming. She landed blows on both Carpenter and Cheng as they came forward, struck their chests and temples and faces, and then she started kicking.

'I won't leave,' she shouted at them. 'Don't even try. I won't leave this room.'

Carpenter staggered as she lashed out. Cheng ducked a kick. Raffaele wondered if they needed to knock her out.

Leanne swung her fists and kicked her legs, screaming. She spat, she cursed, she shook her head violently from side to side.

'Wade in,' Raffaele said. 'Knock her out.'

This only drove Leanne to greater efforts. Her limbs flashed back and forth, warding both Carpenter and Cheng off. Even Raffaele didn't fancy getting in the middle of it. But they had to... wait...

Raffaele reached out and dragged Carpenter away. He thrust his face a little closer to Leanne.

'We're taking you out of here,' he said. 'Whether you like it or nor. Conscious or unconscious. There are three of us and you can't fight us forever. Do you hear me?'

Leanne just growled at him, panting hard. Her eyes were feral.

'But I'll give you an option,' Raffaele said. 'Give us the line of stanza and we'll leave you alone.'

Leanne blinked and stared. She grew calmer, looked Raffaele dead in the eye. She glanced between Carpenter and Cheng.

'Leave me here?' she asked.

'Right here,' Raffaele said. 'No worries.'

She seemed to size them up now, as if wondering if she could trust them. The anger had fallen away from her face, replaced by a kind of placidity. Without another word, she crossed her arms and straightened her legs, laid back on her pillow.

Looking up at the ceiling she said, *'Where Presidents and Generals tarry, drinking champagne.'*

Raffaele tapped her on the shoulder. 'Which line is it?'

'Fourth.'

He grinned and backed away from the woman, holding his hands out. He didn't want to upset her, not now.

We have it, he thought.

CHAPTER SEVENTEEN

Bodie crouched in the shadows with the night pressed all around. It had been a tough decision to wait for the killers.

They had put the psychiatric hospital to their backs, left the area, and then returned on foot, finding positions among the bushes and trees outside from where they could view the comings and goings. They settled in, knowing they were going to be there for hours.

Morally, it wasn't the best decision in the world. This man, Raffaele, would come, and he would find a way to extract the information from Leanne. Bodie had wrestled with it, but had come down firmly on the side of Cassidy. Whatever it took to free her.

They waited. Day turned to night. The hours passed slow and sluggish. They hadn't prepared properly, hadn't brought anything to eat and drink or stave off the cold, but then this wasn't exactly a planned stakeout. They made the best of it.

Bodie and the others weren't exactly sure who they were looking out for, but when the other team turned up, it was a pretty obvious sight. They had been expecting one man – Raffaele – but three turned up. That threw Bodie from the start. But it was the way they moved, the way they stared up at the hospital and made plans, the way they approached it differently to everyone else.

But mostly it was the way they waited from 1 to 8 p.m. for the right time to strike.

It was hell for Bodie and the others. They weren't actually that far away from Raffaele and his friends, and they had to stay still and quiet. Everyone breathed a sigh of relief when the car doors cracked open and the other team moved into the hospital.

Then they waited again. They adjusted their positions slightly, so that they were better able to strike when the time came to it, slightly more in the car's blind spot. They stretched, made ready, tried to shake off the nerves that had been building ever since they'd seen Raffaele.

They didn't know him, but the guy was a supreme killer.

Bodie hated wasting all this time. Every moment they waited, Cassidy was in danger. Who knew what kind of terrible ordeal she was having to endure at the hands of LaRoy? So far, they had two lines of the stanza, including LaRoy's own. It wasn't exactly fast going. Not only that, he knew there would be more gruelling tests ahead.

Finally, the hospital doors opened.

The entire team rose, crouched, made ready without a sound. They tracked the movement of Rafaele and his two colleagues to the car, saw that they were all grinning broadly. A good sign? Bodie thought it was, but not necessarily for Leanne and the staff inside. As they walked, the men spoke to each other in congratulatory tones, and then they heard Raffaele tell them – Carpenter and Cheng – to keep the chatter to a minimum.

Raffaele put his hand on the car door. Bodie and his team leapt from the shadows. They attacked the three men like striking snakes, hitting hard. Bodie took Raffaele, smashing a fist into the back of the man's neck, trying to incapacitate him with one hit. Raffaele slammed forward from the impact, forehead colliding with the top of the car. Bodie had expected him to stagger, maybe slump, but the figure just lashed out, throwing elbows left and right. There was a splash of blood from where his forehead had hit the car.

Yasmine took Carpenter, kicked at the backs of his legs to unbalance him, and then hooked an arm around his neck. She squeezed hard, pulled him in close. Carpenter kicked and struggled and tried to twist around.

He succeeded, surprisingly strong. Yasmine was now face to face with the man. She drove a knee into his abdomen, an elbow to his face. This time, he staggered away, gasping.

Reilly hit Cheng from the side, elbows first, rushing in hard and not slowing down. Cheng bounced off him, hitting the car and falling to his knees. Reilly didn't slow; he struck Cheng again, sending him back against the car, his head striking with a heavy sound. Cheng's eyes rolled, his limbs went momentarily limp.

Heidi, Jemma and Lucie were spare, though Lucie wasn't a fighter. Heidi thought it was Bodie who might need the help, because of the class of fighter that he faced, and she wasn't wrong. Despite Bodie's powerful attack, Raffaele was already fighting back with no discernible decrease in faculties.

Heidi ran around to that side of the car.

Raffaele punched and kicked out at Bodie, driving him away. His forehead was bleeding. Under the stark light, the two figures fought back and forth across the otherwise dark car park.

Heidi ran in at Raffaele from behind. She swept his legs away, sending him tumbling. Raffaele hit the asphalt hard, smashed a cheekbone into the ground and left more blood behind. Then he rolled, kicked out, came up with an acrobatic leap, and spun immediately into a spinning side kick.

The kick caught Bodie across the chin, sending him instantly to the ground where he lay groaning. Heidi suddenly faced Raffaele alone.

'You should not have challenged me.'

Heidi didn't respond. Instead, she circled Raffaele, giving Bodie all the time she could to recover. Raffaele saw her tactic.

'Not good enough,' he said.

He sprang at her, came down with hands and elbows whirling. Heidi took a smack to the temple, another to the nose, and staggered.

Bodie rose to his knees, shaking his head.

Reilly was working hard to subdue Cheng. He kneed the guy in the face as he sat on the ground, grabbed his head and slammed it against the car. Cheng gasped in agony, face screwing up. Reilly threw him to the floor, jumped on his stomach, knees first. He threw two wild punches, connecting with Cheng's ears, and saw, in his face, a lot of the fight go out of the man.

But they were here for one reason only.

Reilly grabbed the man around the neck and leaned in.

'What's the line?' he whispered harshly. 'Tell me now or you'll never wake up.'

He didn't let up at first, but squeezed more tightly. He wanted Cheng to feel how helpless he really was. The guy's eyes bulged, his mouth worked.

Reilly shifted his hands slightly.

Hierarchy of Madness

'You ready to talk?'

'Go fu-'

Reilly slapped him this time before returning his clenched hands to the man's neck. He had no qualms about doing it. Cheng would have done worse to Leanne and the staff inside if he'd had to.

'Ready to talk yet?' he tried again.

Cheng lashed out at him.

Yasmine was in a similar situation with Carpenter. She pummelled and kicked him, smashing him back repeatedly against the car, each blow targeting a sensitive area. Carpenter's head was hanging. He looked punch drunk.

'We want the line you took from Leanne,' she said as Carpenter rolled close to her. 'Tell me and I'll stop.'

Carpenter swung at her, telegraphing the blow a mile away. Yasmine ducked it and then struck again, making her attacks telling. Carpenter winced and gasped and looked like he wanted to curl up.

Heidi backed away as Raffaele came at her. He was ridiculously quick and every blow that he landed hurt like hell. His face was implacable, his eyes shining as if he was in his element. He leapt at her...

... but didn't see Bodie half rise and kick out. Bodie's blow hit Raffaele on the thigh and unbalanced him. The man landed in an ungainly heap on the floor. As he did so, he seemed to remember his men. He looked over at them.

'Go!' he yelled. 'Run! You must run!'

It made Reilly double down. If he rained enough pain down on his adversary, it would force the man to give up his secret. Reilly didn't hit to debilitate, he hit soft spots to make it hurt.

'Please,' Cheng whispered.

'Give me the line.'

Cheng was hidden from Raffaele's sight behind the car wheel. His head was practically rubbing up against it. He licked split lips and glared up at Reilly through bloodshot eyes.

'I... can't...'

Reilly broke his nose. Cheng wailed. Reilly smashed the man hard in the broken nose, prepared to do it again.

'Stop,' Cheng, helpless, moaned.

'It's only gonna get worse from here.'

'All right. *Listen.* It's all a load of crap. It's *where Presidents and Generals tarry, drinking champagne.* That's all. Means nothing. It's-'

'Shut up,' Reilly punched him in the gut.

And jumped swiftly to his feet. 'I have it!' he yelled.

CHAPTER EIGHTEEN

Bodie put his foot down hard on the gas as they roared away from the hospital.

As soon as Reilly shouted that he'd got the line they had disengaged, run away from the fight. They'd raced to their car, jumped inside, and sped off. They were desperate; ragged and frantic with worry. Anything went when it came to getting Cassidy back.

So they'd left Raffaele and his minions behind, not caring that they were on top, not worried about anything but getting the line of the stanza.

And now they had three.

Bodie drove through the night, at first driving aimlessly. Then he pulled in, let Reilly take over, and pulled the burner cell from his pocket.

'You calling him?' Heidi asked.

'We have three lines of the stanza,' Bodie said. 'We need to know where to go next.'

They were battered and bruised. Heidi had bent a finger back so that it throbbed constantly and Yasmine's ribs hurt. She didn't think any were broken, but they were definitely sore and painful.

Bodie made the call.

'Again you call me in the dead of night,' LaRoy answered almost immediately. 'Are you doing it on purpose?'

'Put Cassidy on,' Bodie said.

'Luckily for you, I am with her as we speak. Keeping her company. She loves it. Now, Cassidy dear, let your Bodie know you are alive and well.'

'Fuck you,' Bodie heard the redhead's voice.

'There you have it,' LaRoy said. 'There's your proof. Now, what do you have for me?'

Bodie stared into the darkness that passed to either side of the car. 'Look,' he said. 'There was another team once again. They almost beat us to it. What kind of operation are you running?'

LaRoy grumbled almost silently. 'There are holes in my operation. As I told you, I am trying to plug them.'

'Well, try harder. Someone is playing you, and they have all the same knowledge that you're giving us.'

'I have narrowed down the field of traitors.'

'Good. Let's hear them.' Bodie thought the information might be useful.

'That is none of your concern. Now, you have Leanne's line of stanza. That makes three. Let me hear them.'

Bodie raised an eyebrow, thinking. 'You have your line. Antonio's line. And now Leanne's line. That's lines one, three and four. *"A Ghost Town famous in the nineteenth century;*

the Eighteen Million Dollar Goldmine, where Presidents and Generals tarry, drinking champagne."'

LaRoy took it all in, not speaking for several minutes. 'That tells us precisely jack shit.'

'It's barely researchable,' Lucie said.

Bodie repeated the three lines again, waiting for LaRoy to say something more.

'It brings us to the next family member,' the man said finally. 'Gary LaRoy. The recluse.'

'What information do you have for us?' Bodie asked.

'A good question. As I said, Gary is a recluse.'
Bodie blinked in the dark. 'You must have something.'
'He's close to the Dexter marsh. There are sightings of Gary in the nearby town of Limerick, Dexter, itself, and the Black Bay Marsh camping ground. These sightings are infrequent, as you can imagine. My guess is, he lives in the marshes.'
'The Dexter Marsh lies at the eastern end of Lake Ontario, in Dexter, New York.' Lucie was already researching the place. 'Limerick is less than two miles away. You think this area is Gary LaRoy's... stomping ground?'
'I know it is. I'm certain.'
'How can you be so sure?'
'Please listen. I already told you. I keep tabs on them. Gary's been spotted several times through the years buying equipment and eating occasionally in the cafes. The first spot was pure luck, I admit, but ever since then I have had men and women occasionally patrolling the entire area, getting me a good spot of Gary. It takes time... but he does appear.'
'And this recluse has a cabin in the woods? How are we supposed to find that?' Heidi asked.
'That's your problem, but I suggest you make it quick. For Cassidy's sake. She's easy on the eyes, but hard as nails on the ears.'
Bodie felt his muscles clench as he thought about what he wanted to do to LaRoy. 'Lay one finger on her and I'll-'
'Oh, it's a little late for that, Bodie, but she'll live. I think. She'll never be the same, but she'll live.'
Bodie closed his eyes momentarily. Then he spoke again when he thought he could manage a little civility. 'Listen to me-'

'Oh, don't worry, I'm jesting with you. The blood's barely noticeable. The bones will knit. Her eyes... I'm not so sure.' LaRoy broke out into a fit of laughter.

'If you want us to help you, keep her in good shape,' Bodie grated. 'I want photographs.'

'Just do your damn job.'

The call ended abruptly. Bodie stared at the phone, gritting his teeth. He wanted to throw it against the dash, but knew what a stupid idea that would be. Reilly, in the driving seat, glanced over at him.

'We'll get her back safe,' he said.

Bodie was thankful for the effort, but he knew better than anyone how deep LaRoy's madness ran. Even if they got all seven lines of the stanza, even if they delivered them to LaRoy, *even if they located the gemstones,* he doubted LaRoy would let Cassidy live. He had no reason to think that way. Not yet. But Bodie was nothing if he wasn't practical.

'You think he's going to kill her, don't you?' Heidi said.

Bodie swivelled to look at her. 'I think we need something else other than all seven lines of the stanza.'

'Leverage,' Lucie said. 'But what?'

'It's something to think about,' Yasmine said. 'But where are we going right now?'

Bodie heard her words and, with a tremendous struggle, forced himself to consider their current situation. They were already in upstate New York.

'Lucie?' he asked, knowing that she'd already be researching.

'It's a three-hour drive,' she said.

'We're lucky the family members have stuck to the general area where they were born,' Heidi said. 'I guess they still feel close to their birthplace.'

'Don't jinx it,' Bodie said.

They programmed the new route into the sat nav and set off, following the single blue line on the map. The arrival time was a little after two in the morning, but that didn't bother them. If there wasn't a hotel available, they'd stay in the car for the night.

Lucie started making the appropriate calls.

They drove through the dark night in tense silence. Bodie noticed that Reilly and Yasmine were exchanging looks in the rearview mirror and wondered if the two were trying to rekindle their old relationship. He took the time to glance at Heidi, tried to read what was in her eyes. She didn't look away, didn't smile, didn't actually give him any sign that she cared for him. Maybe she was worried about Cass.

It had been a whirlwind few days. Whatever personal dilemmas or comforts they were currently experiencing had been rightly shelved. Nothing mattered apart from Cassidy's safe return. But that still left several unresolved struggles on the table.

Bodie now had time to think. None of them could do anything else until they arrived in Dexter, and daybreak rose. It was a time when he might have spoken to Heidi, when he might have asked her a few relevant questions. Maybe Reilly and Yasmine were feeling the same. But, as always for Bodie, life got in the way.

They drove southeast, following the NY-11B and then a series of other roads until they came to the NY-180 that would lead them into Dexter. By that time, they were all tired, aching from the fight and swallowing painkillers. They'd stopped at a service station and bought on-the-road supplies, including water, soda, sandwiches and candy. Painkillers and bandages, too. Yasmine spent some time wrapping her ribs in the back of the car. Bodie had bought some extra strong cloth tape because, on kicking Raffaele, he'd strained the tendons in his right big toe. He spent some time strapping the toe to its mate and hoping that helped alleviate the pain.

Dexter is a small town in Jefferson county, adjacent to the Black River, a tributary of Lake Ontario. It had a wide downtown main street with pleasant buildings on both sides and plenty of parking spaces. The team found the hotel Lucie had booked and parked right outside, tired, spent, and happy to trudge to their rooms.

Their heads were down.

Later that morning, they would begin the search for Gary LaRoy.

HIERARCHY OF MADNESS

CHAPTER NINETEEN

A bright sun welcomed them as they stepped out of the hotel and into the morning. Dexter's paved streets were bathed in it. The team stuck together and followed Google Maps on their way to the first hardware store on their list. They figured they'd hit all the hardware stores, along with camping goods stores, convenience stores and a few others they thought Gary might use when he needed to.

That morning, LaRoy had sent them through his most recent picture of Gary. He was a tall, broad-shouldered individual with long white hair and a bristly white beard. He wore a lumberjack shirt and jeans and old, battered boots. His skin was wrinkled prematurely, Bodie thought, maybe because of his lifestyle, maybe because of other earlier reasons in his life. Bodie didn't blame the man for wanting to get away.

It was a luckless quest. They split up, sent the picture to each other's phones. They asked for their friend, Gary, figuring he'd frequent Dexter as much as he'd go to any other local town. They tried locksmiths, a bait shop, a neighbourhood market, a butcher, a grocery store. It was Lucie's idea to try the post office.

It was the middle of the afternoon before they got there and their feet ached; they were tired of traipsing around. They waited until the store was empty and then Bodie and Heidi wandered inside, went up to the counter, arm in arm, and smiled at a blonde-haired lady wearing square glasses, a necktie and a large wedding ring. The lady smiled widely at them, revealing teeth almost as white as Bodie's.

Heidi stepped up first. 'Oh, hi,' she said in a pleasant voice. 'We're here in town for a few days and just thought we'd look up an old friend, maybe surprise him. We have no idea where he lives and wondered if you could point us in the right direction?'

The woman's eyebrows went up. She squinted hard at the photo. 'What's your friend's name?' she asked.

'Gary,' Bodie said. 'Gary LaRoy.'

'That's Gary alright, and he comes in here occasionally. But I can't just give you his address. You know why.'

Bodie did, indeed. Government employees would be forbidden from giving out addresses. But short of camping out outside the store and waiting for what might be weeks, he didn't see any alternative. He wondered if the store kept records of its customers' addresses.

Probably not.

'It would really help us out,' he said.

'I am sorry, but I can't help you.' The woman's eyes turned hard.

Bodie thanked her and the two exited the store. The others were waiting for them out on the street.

'Gary lives around here,' Bodie said. 'He's known at the post office. But they won't give us his address.'

'We didn't expect them to,' Lucie said. 'Now that we know he comes here, there is more than one way to skin a rabbit.'

Bodie looked at her, eyes wide. What was she thinking? She looked back at him and grinned. 'The watering hole,' she said.

HIERARCHY OF MADNESS

Bodie thought about it and, yes, it made sense. Even if Gary never went near the place, there would be some people who knew him. And perhaps one of them was getting drunk at this time of day.

'Shall we all go?' he said.

'I know I want to,' Yasmine said. 'But let's try more than one at once,' she immediately linked arms with Reilly.

Bodie chose Heidi. Jemma and Lucie decided to walk in together. As couples, they crossed the road, walked down the street for a few minutes, and then entered the pubs. Yasmine and Reilly chose the first, Bodie and Heidi the second. Lucie and Jemma found a third further along the main street.

Bodie slowed when he got inside, letting his eyes adjust to the dimness, his body to the cool air conditioning. He saw a seating area to the left, a bar to the right. Several men were propping the bar up, pint glasses standing before them. None of them turned around to check who'd entered the bar.

The barman stared at them. 'Help you?'

Bodie figured they may as well start off strong. He also figured he might as well tell a closer version of the truth.

'We're looking for an old friend. Gary LaRoy. Moved up this way quite a few years ago and we've lost touch. I was wondering if you might help us out.'

The barman shrugged and then looked at the photo on Bodie's phone. His eyes narrowed.

'That's not Gary LaRoy,' he said. 'It's Gary Browning.'

Bodie felt his heart leap. 'Then maybe keep that piece of information to yourself.'

The barman eyed them. 'Gary's a loner. Doesn't

come in here often. When he does, it's for a few whiskeys to ward off the cold. Takes a bottle away with him. Doesn't talk much. I've never seen him with anyone else.'

'Do you know where he lives?'

The barman picked up a glass and started cleaning it with a cloth. He did it until the glass shone, all the while evaluating Bodie and Heidi. Finally, he gave them a shake of his head.

'I don't think that's the right thing to do.'

Heidi took out her purse, showed the barman a wedge of greenbacks.

'The man's a recluse,' the barman said hesitantly. 'Self imposed. How did you say you knew him again?'

'New York,' Heidi said before Bodie's English accent caused them even more trouble. 'I went to the same school as him. We grew up together. I always knew he came up this way and I kind of want to know what happened to him.'

'I can't help you,' the barman said loudly.

But with a quick jerk of his head, he sent them to the very end of the bar, away from any flapping ears.

'Listen,' he whispered. 'I don't like this, but you two look like you're on the level. Let me see some of that wad.'

Heidi plucked five twenties from her stash and placed it on the bar. 'It's worth it to me,' she said.

The barman was still wavering. He stared at the money and then at Bodie and Heidi, studying their eyes. The thought of giving them Gary's address clearly didn't sit well with him.

'I don't know the exact place,' he said. 'It's out of town. I know the general area. It's among the marshlands.'

'Marshlands?' Heidi didn't like the sound of that.

'Yeah, on account of the Black River. We got a lot of marshes around here. Easy to get lost in.'

'But Gary lives in them?' Heidi sounded surprised.

'Not the guy you remember?' the barman asked.

Heidi tried to get back on track. 'Is it easy to find these marshlands?'

'Easy enough. There's a dirt road between the grocery store and Maisie's pharmacy. Follow it for a while and you're in the marshes. There's an old silo to your right half a mile or so further down and then...' he stopped suddenly, realising what he'd been doing.

'We're not bad people,' Bodie said.

Heidi flashed the cash again. 'Is it worth your while?'

The bar tender's eyes fixed greedily on the money. He bit his lower lip, grabbed another glass and began polishing it furiously, as if to take his mind off the dilemma. He didn't look at them for a while, but then raised his eyes.

'Hand it over,' he said.

'Finish the directions,' Heidi returned.

'Don't worry, I'll tell you. Go past the old grain silo – don't go inside, it's treacherous – and follow a branch to the right. That should take you to Gary's front door. I don't like it.' he shook his head. 'But money talks. Oh, and one other thing – Gary likes guns.'

Bodie stared. 'Are you warning us off?'

'I'm saying that's fair warning.'

'Is he the kind of guy who shoots first?' Heidi asked.

'Every time.'

Bodie thanked the barman and turned to leave the premises. Heidi doled out the money and then followed. The two of them found the others in the street.

'Any luck?' Reilly asked.

'I'd say, yes,' Heidi told him, looking up and down the long sunlit street with its tan frontages and paved roads and well-trimmed stands of trees. She screwed her face up. 'Maybe,' she said.

'I'd say it's a bit of a good news, bad news scenario,' Bodie said.

'And I'd say that's playing it down,' Heidi said. 'This guy has guns.'

CHAPTER TWENTY

It wasn't difficult to find a path through the marshlands. There was an awful lot of water around, and they were conscious of walking towards the fast flowing Black River, but they walked the path between the two stores, found the old grain silo and then continued along the branch to the right.

They walked as a group, but warily, wondering if they were going to meet Gary somewhere en route to his cabin, most of all wondering how he might react. The guy was a recluse and here they were, six-strong, strolling in to have a chat.

The sun rode the sky brightly, bearing down on them, but a fresh breeze across the marshlands cooled everything to a manageable level. Bodie saw dark birds rising and falling, wheeling across the skies. He heard the pad of animals, the low cadence of insects all around. The marshes overgrew the path, but they pushed their way through without deviating.

Bodie enjoyed the bracing walk. He didn't enjoy the tension that settled over them, that gnawed at his soul. It wasn't just the approach; it was the worry for Cassidy, the constant knowledge that she was in the hands of a killer, a killer who was making the relic hunters dance to his tune.

Finally, as midday approached and then went by, they saw a long ramshackle building ahead. It was a bit of a mishmash, as if someone had kept adding to the place long after they built it. Logs made up the walls, and there was a red-tiled roof that went to an apex.

Reilly nodded at the half-ajar wooden front door. 'You think he's expecting someone?'

'A recluse?' Yasmine returned. 'I doubt it.'

'Could be a distraction,' Bodie said. 'Let's not risk it.'

They started shouting Gary's name, making their presence known. Their voices rang out across the marshes, scaring a flock of birds that took flight with a thunder of wings. There were pools of water to left and right, a wide creek running ahead, and a deep ditch that led past the recluse's front door. Bodie's first thought was that he wouldn't fancy negotiating that on a dark, drunken night.

There was no reply. No movement. Maybe Gary was trying to wait them out.

They tried again, voices raised. They had no intentions of approaching the large hut. Bodie made sure they were all in plain sight.

It went on for half an hour. In the end, they stopped because their voices were becoming hoarse. Bodie looked around at the team, shrugged.

'What the hell do we do now?'

'We don't leave,' Lucie said. 'He'll have to come out eventually.'

As she spoke, something moved out of the corner of Bodie's eye. It wasn't a vast movement, just a shift, but it came from the doorway. When he focused, he saw the gleam of a double-barrel shotgun poking out.

'We just want to talk,' he yelled quickly. 'A quick conversation.'

'Go away,' the man spoke in a dull monotone, and then pulled a trigger. The sound of the shotgun going off made Bodie jump, and he was thankful the guy had aimed over the marshes. Now, hundreds of birds took flight and there was the quick sound of things scuttling away.

'Ten minutes,' Lucie persisted. 'And we're gone.'

More movement. They could now see the man in the picture they'd been sent, the tall, broad-shouldered man with long white hair and a bristly white beard. Even now he wore a lumberjack shirt and jeans and old, battered boots. His face was a mass of wrinkles. The man advanced through the door and out onto the wooden porch. Now he levelled the shotgun at them.

'She still has one shot left,' he said. 'Which one of you shitbirds wants it?' And he shook his pocket so that it rattled. 'Still got a lot of spares too, for the rest.'

'Mr... Browning, is it?' Heidi took a tentative step forward. 'Could we please have ten minutes of your time? It's very important.'

'Important to *you*. Not important to me. I couldn't give a shit. Now, turn your asses around and hightail it back the way you came.'

'You really going to shoot us?' Yasmine asked with her hands on her hips.

Now Gary looked a little unsure. 'You're on my property.'

'You own the marshes?'

'That ain't the point.'

'Ten minutes,' Bodie said.

'What the hell kind of accent is that?'

Bodie didn't answer, just held his ground. There was a long silence between them, in which the only sound was the flapping of returning birds and the flow of the distant river. Bodie betrayed no emotions, but inside he was getting desperate.

'Shit,' the recluse finally said, and then waved his gun at them. 'You're just gonna stand right there, aren't you?'

They all nodded. *Yes.*

'So talk. What the hell do you want?'

Bodie's bare arms were covered in beads of sweat. He wiped his forehead. 'That's the hard part,' he said. 'Any chance you could put that gun down?'

Gary stared at them, looked left and right and off into the marshes. Then, he lowered the gun, pointed its business end at the ground and sniffed. 'That'll have to be good enough,' he said.

Bodie approached him until they were about ten feet apart. His gaze never left Gary's own. With a wave, he told the others to stay back.

Heidi went with him.

Together, they confronted Gary. Bodie took a deep breath.

'First, I want you to know that, once this conversation's done, you'll never see us again. All we want is a little information. We don't want anything else from you.'

'How'd you find me?'

Bodie braced himself. 'Your brother,' he said. 'Manny LaRoy.'

This was the moment of truth. Gary could suddenly turn many ways. Bodie held his breath, prepared to dive for the gun hand.

'Never heard of him,' Gary sniffed.

'We know you're Gary LaRoy,' Heidi said. 'We know all about your family, your father. It's your father who has caused this.'

'I still don't understand how you found me.'

'Manny kept tabs on all of you. He's that kind of guy.

Hierarchy of Madness

Because, he knew, that one day he might need you again.'

Gary looked around him at the marshes, at the dirt paths, at the ditches and streams and puddles. 'A guy really can't disappear, can he?'

Bodie nodded. 'You can. Just give us a piece of information and you'll never see us again.'

'I enjoy living here,' Gary said distractedly. 'I don't like people.'

Bodie saw the gun arm twitch.

'If you shoot us, you'll go to jail,' Heidi said. 'You'll enjoy that a lot less.'

Gary glared at them. 'Ask me what you want,' he said, and then took a long look back at the hut as if missing its quiet solitude.

'Your father gave you a line of a stanza,' Bodie said after taking a deep breath. 'The LaRoy family stanza, he called it. It's simple enough. We need the line he gave you.'

Gary LaRoy stared at them. 'You fixing to go grab those gemstones?'

'Not exactly,' Bodie said, wondering just how much to reveal to get this man to help them. 'Manny is forcing us to work for him.'

Gary blinked. His eyes went distant, as if a sudden recollection had hit him. He opened his mouth once, closed it, then opened it again.

'Manny always was a bastard,' he said.

'I agree,' Bodie nodded. 'Is there any chance you could give us that line?'

Gary let the gun fall to the ground, rubbed his face, and came a step closer. He was no longer a threat, and he looked tired, older than his years. 'I came out here to escape all that,' he said. 'Family. It was never good for me. It never fit. If you got yourselves a good family, keep it. Hold on to it. Do anything. Cos if you get yourself a bad one...' Gary shuddered.

'We have a good family,' Bodie said.

'That's what this is all about then,' Gary said. 'Family, good and bad. There's ours, rotten to the core, and you have yours. Will you risk yours against ours?'

Bodie hadn't seen it that way. Now, he saw that LaRoy's family had split *his* apart and there was only one way forward. 'I'm all in,' he said. 'I have to be. Manny LaRoy is threatening everything we hold dear.'

Gary kicked at the ground. He nodded. 'I assumed as much, and I'm sorry for you. Our father was the biggest bastard of all. He made us this way, made me want to leave everything behind. But Manny wasn't far behind him. He got used to the turmoil and the trauma. He eventually revelled in it.'

'I believe he still does,' Heidi said.

'My line? Listen up. *I see diamonds, gold, the richest gemstones.*'

Bodie tried not to look disappointed. 'Is that it?'

'Yeah, I know I'm the worst son. I got the shoddiest line.'

'Believe me, it's not the worst,' Bodie said. 'Which line is it?'

'Five. Can I go back to my life now?'

Bodie thanked the man and turned on his heel. He watched Gary pick up the gun and then trudge back into his hut. He walked back to the others.

'We have lines one, three, four and five,' he said. 'And we have nothing. I'm wondering if this isn't a wild goose chase.'

Heidi was at his shoulder. 'It can't be,' she said. 'Maybe the directions come in the last two lines.'

'I bloody well hope so.'

'I think we assume they do,' Reilly said. 'We still have three LaRoys' to visit. That's almost half the stanza.'

Bodie looked up to the sky. He was tired. The sun warmed him, but it didn't revitalise him. Nothing would... until Cassidy was safe.

'We go again,' he said. 'We move on.'

As a team, they turned away from Gary's hut and started making their way back through the marshlands. It wouldn't take long. Their car was probably a half hour away, maybe less. It was as he walked down the dirt path that Bodie saw movement ahead. There were figures coming up the path.

'Hide,' he whispered suddenly.

'Crap, is that Raffaele?' Lucie asked.

Bodie nodded. 'And his goons or two more,' he said.

'They're coming for Gary,' Reilly said.

'We can't let that happen,' Bodie said.

'The old man can take care of himself,' Yasmine said.

But Bodie liked the man, felt for him after hearing about the family issues. There was a point in his life, when his mother and father had been killed, that Bodie felt the same.

'We stop them,' he said. 'Before they reach Gary.'

They raced into the rushes by the side of the road, losing themselves in the long grass and treading cautiously. They were careful to avoid puddles and small streams. From here, crouching, they could see the approach of Raffaele and his men. This time, there were two new individuals with the killer. Maybe the other two had been sent back in shame after the last battle. Raffaele and his goons were just passing the old grain silo, keeping it to their right and walking down the very centre of the dirt path. Bodie made his way through the long grasses until they were level in the road with them.

'We end this here,' he said. 'I can't do with someone following our every move. Not where Cassidy's safety is paramount.'

'What if they're armed?' Reilly said.

'That's what shock and awe are for,' Bodie told him. 'You ready?'

'You're fucking crazy, dude,' Reilly said.

Bodie knew that was one way of looking at it. The other way was that Gary had taken nothing from his life; he'd been given nothing. He didn't deserve a killer like Raffaele.

'Move,' he said.

CHAPTER TWENTY ONE

Bodie shot out of the long grasses just as Raffaele and his two men came alongside. He was running fast, hard, leading with his shoulder, and he smashed into the nearest man with full force. This guy had flowing locks and a long face and a dusting of facial hair. He didn't see Bodie coming and went sideways, crashing into his friend who was the total opposite in looks – short-cropped hair and nothing on his pudgy face except an often broken nose. He looked like a boxer.

The first guy slammed into the second guy. Both went flying. Raffaele was behind them, eyes wide, a shocked look on his face.

The rest of the relic hunters were a step behind Bodie.

Reilly and Yasmine targeted the killer. Heidi threw herself past Bodie and tackled the second man. Bodie recovered from his own blow and punched at the throat, but his opponent retained the presence of mind to turn away even as he fell to his knees.

Bodie didn't stand on any ceremony. He used his knees, smashing them into the back of the guy's head and neck, giving him no quarter. The man fell even further down, holding himself up by flinging his hands out. Bodie kicked at the ribs and then the skull, not letting up.

Beyond him, Heidi had punched her opponent in the

ribs as he staggered. Now she kicked at his legs, making him completely lose his balance. He ended up in the dirt, and she fell on top of him, trying to capture his arms with her knees, raining blows down that he tried to dodge.

Reilly feinted left and right, watching Raffaele carefully. In a moment, the killer had whisked out a small knife, a fillet knife, that he held underhand confidently, waiting for them to approach.

Reilly waded in, leapt aside as the knife flashed. He had been ready for it. Yasmine struck from the other side, catching Raffaele cross the cheek. The killer grunted, came again, flashing the knife at both of them with two wide slices.

Reilly felt to the floor, kicked out at Raffaele's legs. The manoeuvre surprised the other man. He had no answer to it. His legs buckled, and he swayed. Yasmine struck at him.

Bodie pummelled his opponent until the guy stopped moving. He knelt on the man's back, wished he had some zip ties, but knew knocking him out cold was as good as it was going to get. He delivered a few more kicks to make sure the guy was properly comatose and then rose to help Heidi.

The curly-haired woman was kneeling atop her opponent, but he was struggling massively. She could barely keep her seat and was concentrating on raining blows down at his neck and temples. The guy heaved, lifting himself partway off the ground and Heidi into the air. Then he twisted, trying to buck her off.

Bodie stamped on one hand, making him collapse, and then kicked him in the side of the head. The guy groaned, slumped. Heidi kept on punching. With a last effort, the guy reared up, twisted and threw her off.

Bodie stepped in, but the man was tougher than he appeared. He scooted around in the dirt, sweeping his legs out, and took Bodie's own legs out from under him. Bodie landed on his tailbone, the pain shooting through his body.

Raffaele staggered backwards into the rushes, the huge shape of the old grain silo at his back. His right foot came down in water and mud, made him slip. He warded them off with a sweep of his knife. Reilly and Yasmine made sure they approached him from two different angles.

'Give it up,' Reilly said. 'Leave here.'

'Is that all you want?'

'What do you want with us?' Yasmine figured they'd try to distract the man, play dumb for a while.

'I don't want *you*, fool. I want something else.'

Raffaele came at them now, flicking the shining blade in both their directions. It sliced the air apart an inch from Reilly's nose, parted the cloth of Yasmine's jacket. Raffaele didn't stop, just came forward, shifting the knife around.

Reilly and Yasmine backed up along the dirt path.

Raffaele's eyes flicked to his two comrades. Clearly, he would see that they were in dire straits. His face betrayed nothing.

Yasmine decided she would keep him talking until their own colleagues could come to help. 'What happened to Carpenter and Cheng?'

Raffaele spat. 'They weren't cut out for this business.'

'Did you kill them?'

'I wish. Maybe another time.'

Raffaele swung again. Reilly avoided the blow and stepped in, knocking the knife arm away. This gave

Yasmine the opportunity to deliver a stunning blow to Raffaele's nose. She broke it. The blood started flowing.

'Time to give it up,' she said.

'Time for you to die,' Raffaele said. Ignoring his nose, he came forward.

Bodie tried to roll out of the way, but his opponent followed, sending out a few debilitating kicks of his own. Bodie caught one in the spine and another in the meat of his thigh and felt the latter muscle go dead. Pain crawled through his body, travelling from top to bottom, blossoming like blood flow. He scuttled away, trying to evade the kicks.

But his opponent was enjoying it too much. There was a twisted grin on his face. In fact, he was enjoying it so much that he didn't notice Heidi rear up on his blind side and smash a rotten log across the back of his neck.

The log shattered instantly, sending chunks and splinters of wood in all directions. The attacker stumbled forward under the impact and then fell over Bodie, collapsing face first to the ground. Bodie tried to stand, but his dead leg wouldn't let him. Instead, he crawled over to his opponent, used the man's own jacket to drag himself into a face-to-face position.

Bodie head-butted him.

The guy fell away dramatically, nose exploding. By that time Heidi was also upon him, and punched him three more times on the way down. Her own knuckles were bleeding by now, cut and scratched.

The man was laid out, sprawling, as comatose as his friend.

Bodie rubbed his thigh frantically, trying to get the feeling back into the muscle. He knew Reilly and Yasmine needed their help, knew that the more people

facing Raffaele, the better it would go for them.
Heidi hauled him to his feet.
Bodie limped over towards Raffaele. The killer was holding his own against both Reilly and Yasmine. Bodie wanted to see what would happen when he added himself and Heidi to the mix. With a jerk of his head, he indicated that Jemma and Lucie should watch the two fallen men.

'Shout if they move,' he said.

Raffaele lashed out at Reilly, moved instantly into another pose, and struck Yasmine on the right leg. Both staggered. Bodie, with his dead thigh, didn't feel like much help, but he ran in anyway.

Raffaele saw him coming, span on the spot, and delivered a kick to Bodie's chest. It sent him flying backwards into the oncoming Heidi. Bodie couldn't help falling to the floor. Raffaele didn't stop moving.

The killer lashed out at Reilly, catching him in the throat. He span low, tripping Yasmine. Bodie scrambled to his feet, aching. By the time he was face to face with Raffaele again, the man was in a different position entirely, coming at Bodie from the left. Heidi was on her knees and had to throw herself back down to the ground to avoid a blow. Bodie blocked a knee strike that still rocked him backward.

But despite all his efforts, Raffaele was still in the same position. One man against four opponents. And he was tiring. Bodie could see his chest heaving.

Just then, there was a shout from Lucie and Jemma. Bodie turned to see the Raffaele's colleagues struggling to their feet. Raffaele backed away, eyes everywhere. Something unseen and unheard seemed to pass between the three bad guys and, suddenly, they were in flight.

They were legging it, Bodie saw, running straight for the grain silo. He watched them go, panting, letting his body take a break. No way was he running after them. They'd got what they came for. Quickly, he turned to Jemma and Lucie.

'Quick. Run back and warn Gary. We'll wait here for you.'

They stood in the sun, watching and waiting. After several minutes, from the grain silo, there came a tremendous noise and a loud scream. Bodie remembered they'd been warned it was a dangerous place.

Maybe the silo had done them a favour.

Soon, Jemma and Lucie were back, reporting they Gary didn't seem too bothered about the extra company and wasn't inclined to heed their warnings. Bodie could do nothing except lead the way back to town and back to their car.

Behind them, the marshlands remained quiet for a while.

CHAPTER TWENTY TWO

Bodie made the call.

'LaRoy,' he said. 'We now have four lines of the stanza.'

'That's good,' came the faraway, crackly voice. 'Which line did he have?'

'The fifth. It goes: *"I see diamonds, gold, the richest gemstones."*'

'Another line that means nothing,' LaRoy swore.

'Have you ever given any thought,' Bodie said carefully. 'To the possibility that your father might have given everyone meaningless lines? That this may all be a cruel joke?'

The long silence told Bodie that LaRoy had *not* considered that possibility. He waited, sitting in the car, now twenty miles east of Dexter.

'No,' he said finally. 'No. That can't be it. Father was cruel, but he wouldn't go through all that effort for nothing. And I know he purchased the gemstones. If not hidden, where else could they be? And I think Cassidy hopes the stanza proves useful. Isn't that right, my darling?'

There was a muffled curse. Bodie was glad to hear it. It proved Cassidy was still herself, still fighting.

'We all hope it's useful,' he said, mollifying the man. 'I'm sure the next three lines will tell all.'

LaRoy could be heard mumbling something to

Cassidy. This time, there was no reply. Bodie wanted to take the man's attention away from the redhead, even if it was just for a few minutes.

'What next?' he asked tiredly. 'What's next, LaRoy?'

'You're moving on to the Jet Setter. This should be interesting.'

'None of this is interesting, you crazy fuck. It's all a madman's folly.'

'Those are dangerous words, Bodie.'

Trouble is, Bodie thought, the guy was right. He had to keep LaRoy as sweet as possible. He changed tack.

'Tell me about this jet setter.'

'Of course. Her name is Paulina LaRoy. She's a party-goer, a socialite, a... flasher of wealth. She gets all around the local New York scene. Knows all the right people. You know what I mean?'

Bodie nodded as Reilly started programming New York into the sat nav. 'I get the general idea.'

'Paulina is totally self-centred. She sees herself as the centre of the universe. Literally. Nobody else in her world matters. That's her madness. The-'

'I think you'll find there are a few people like that,' Lucie said.

'But with Paulina... it goes far beyond obsessive. It's all-encompassing. She doesn't care for anyone, anything. She has no morals, no ethics, no standards other than those she wishes to set for herself. I've always thought, between us all, she is the most likely to be a serial killer because she lacks empathy.'

'Do not tell me she's a serial killer, too,' Yasmine said.

'Not to my knowledge. I only think that she could be a particularly good one.'

Bodie pulled a face, fought hard not to make a retort.

Hierarchy of Madness

This was no time to upset LaRoy. Not again. He waited for the man to continue.

'Get close to Paulina. Ask her for the line. She won't give it up easily.'

Bodie didn't like the sound of that. 'You think?'

'Haven't you been listening? Her very first thoughts will be – what's in it for me? How does it benefit me? So unless you come up with a great idea, be prepared to fail.'

'Do you have her itinerary?' Heidi asked.

'I really don't. But I do know she's going to be at that gala tomorrow night.'

'Gala?'

'At the Met? Don't tell me you don't know the Met?'

'The Metropolitan Museum of Art,' Lucie said. 'I know it well. Two million square feet of floor space. The largest art museum in the U.S. The building is an accumulation of twenty structures–'

'Yes, yes. Well, there's some fancy gala happening tomorrow night. Something about a pretentious painting or artist or whatever. Paulina will be there.'

'And that's where we should contact her?' Bodie asked.

'Can you think of a better way?'

'All right. Send the photo through. We need to know who we're looking for.'

Bodie ended the call quickly, not wanting to give LaRoy the chance to turn the conversation back to Cassidy and her health. Paulina was the fourth out of the six family members that they had to track down, and prying away her line of the stanza wasn't going to be easy. He watched the scenery flash by for a while, refraining from talking.

'Don't you need an invitation to get into a gala?' Jemma asked the question.

'I might be able to help with that,' Lucie said. 'Remember the Atlantis party? We've *headlined* these types of shows.'

'You think they'll let us in on the strength of the relic hunter label?' Heidi said. 'The Atlantis discoveries?'

'I think they'll jump at the chance,' Lucie said.

She got to work on her laptop, crafting an email. Reilly guided the car towards New York. The time had crept past four p.m. by now. The sat nav told them they'd reach their destination by nine. Bodie settled in for a long drive.

Light turned to dark and day turned to night by the time they found a hotel in Manhattan, New York. They left the car in an underground parking garage, checked in, and went straight up to their rooms. Bodie took the opportunity for a quick shower and then ordered room service. He didn't feel like talking to anyone for the rest of the night. He sat on his bed, ate, and thought about Cassidy, about the mission they were on, about how it might end.

How they might *engineer* an ending.

He slept just a couple of hours, thinking long into the night. The hotel all around him was quiet, luxurious, old, as if it too was snoozing. Bodie was up well before dawn, took another shower and went down early for breakfast.

The team met again in the spacious lobby, finding leather couches to sit on and coffee to drink.

'Did you hear from the gala organisers?' Bodie asked Lucie.

'Not yet,' she bit her lip. 'But give them time.'

'We have to plan as if we're going,' Heidi said. 'Tonight. And that we're gonna meet Paulina LaRoy.'

They talked it out, made plans. As the hours passed,

they ventured out to the shops and bought dresses and tuxes and shiny shoes. It didn't help their dwindling funds. They kept the clothes as cheap as possible and then, sometime after eleven, Lucie got a chirp on her phone.

'That's it,' she said, looking at the screen. 'Our invitation has come through.'

'It's on your phone?' Bodie asked.

'Yeah, just show it at the doors, which open at seven.'

'Nice job,' Reilly said.

'I just thought a high-profile event would welcome whoever headlined an event just a few months ago. It's how this world works.'

With hours to kill, the team went their separate ways for a while and did their own thing. Bodie stayed calm and composed, resting where he could. He was ready for six and headed back down to the lobby.

The others filtered down slowly. When he saw Heidi he caught his breath, struck by the way her black dress enhanced her figure and the fake diamonds around her neck sparkled in her eyes.

'You don't scrub up too badly,' he said by way of a compliment.

She eyed him. 'Your bow tie is wonky.'

He smiled. She smiled back. There hadn't been a lot of time for them lately. Whatever they had, it was stuck in limbo, where it had been for quite some time, he thought. But they were professionals, and their friend was in danger. There would be time enough for them later.

They walked the few blocks to the art museum. It was a balmy night, the sun not yet set, the streets jam-packed with traffic. The crowds were thick too, with quite a few people dressed as they were for the gala. Bodie walked along in silence, noting the Met's Fifth Avenue Beaux arts design and the architectural sculpture. Steps led up to the entrances along Fifth, steps that were alive with people milling around, some sitting, some standing.

Bodie saw the main entrance ahead and up to the right. There were men dressed in black suits on the doors, scanning everyone's passes before letting them inside. He turned to Lucie.

'You're up.'

Inside, they passed through the Great Hall into a large gallery where dozens of people were already gathered. At the far end stood a raised dais and podium and several works of art resting on easels. It reminded him of the reason they were supposed to be here.

'Luce,' he said. 'Did you research tonight's artist?'

She looked guilty. 'Nope. I spent all my time on Paulina LaRoy.'

'Let's hope we don't get asked questions,' Bodie saw no reason why they would. 'Anything to tell us on the Paulina front?'

Lucie shrugged. 'Basically, she's a self-centred party animal, as LaRoy told us. Social media is also her game; she's got a few million followers on Instagram. Uses TikTok and the rest of them. Every pic is of her or her and her friends, men, women, you name it. There's just one thing in common with everything she does.'

Yasmine shook her head. 'Which is?'

'*Her*. It's all about Paulina.'

Seven o'clock passed. The gala kicked off. Waiters and waitresses threaded through the throng, silver platters of food and drink in their hands. They spread out a little, searching for Paulina.

The speeches began. A small man with a shock of hair, wearing an expensive suit, took to the stage and started talking about his work. There was a toast and then a recharging of glasses. Bodie's eyes were on everything except the man. He had the image of Paulina LaRoy fixed firmly in his mind. Where the hell was she?

The minutes ticked by. The man on stage started showing off his paintings, eliciting a brief flutter of applause from the audience. As 7.30 ticked past, Bodie entertained the disheartening thought that Paulina might not turn up.

Maybe the gala event wasn't ritzy enough for her.

Maybe she put her name down for every event, but just turned up to the ones that would give her the most visibility. To be fair, he thought, this was rather a minor affair.

The others appeared to be having similar thoughts. They stared at Bodie with gloomy expressions on their faces. But it was as they were all doing this, wondering what to do next, when there was a commotion at the far end of the room and a fashionable figure decided to make a very late unfashionable entrance.

CHAPTER TWENTY THREE

Bodie turned to look.

A woman with long blonde hair, strategic make-up, and wearing a floaty black dress hovered in the doorway. Diamonds sparkled at her ears and neck and were bunched along her wrists. She wore rings larger than Bodie had ever seen and a choker that shone like the sun. She was loud, speaking to someone at her side, suddenly the centre of attention as she pranced into the room.

Bodie recognised the features. This was definitely Paulina.

The woman stalked through the crowd, turning left and right and saying hello to everyone, creating such a commotion and a stir that the diminutive man on stage paused in his speech. She gave him a radiant smile and only stopped when she'd pushed to the front of the crowd. Then, as the man resumed, she turned around and beckoned the serving staff to bring her food and drink.

Bodie thought it cringeworthy. But there was no doubt the woman was highly visible. Even now she was snapping a selfie with the still-talking artist in the background.

'Hurry it along, dear,' Bodie heard her say. 'I have another event to attend after this one.'

For once, he was at a loss. How could they hope to

get a quiet, serious word with this woman? She was the centre of attention, a dazzling light shining on a glittery stage. He looked around as his colleagues approached.

'Any ideas,' he said.

'I say we walk right up to her,' Heidi said. 'Make her notice us.'

'It might be the only way.' Lucie agreed. 'Otherwise, she's gonna grab all the attention in the room.'

Bodie nodded. They sidled their way towards Paulina, waiting for the artist to finish his speech.

Seven minutes later, he wrapped up. Paulina was looking at her phone, scrolling through photos and checking her recent post's progress. She was constantly turning left and right, smiling, rolling her eyes. Whatever worked.

Heidi walked right up to her, leaned in and, before the general hubbub could rise around the room, spoke four words.

'Manny LaRoy sent us.'

Paulina froze, the smile plastered on her face. She didn't turn, but stared fixedly at the artist on the stage in front of her. The man was now talking to a select group of people about a particular painting.

Heidi frowned. Bodie didn't pretend to know how Paulina's mind worked, but maybe shutting someone down helped her concentrate on herself.

'Manny LaRoy sent us,' Heidi said again, this time a little louder.

Paulina still didn't react. She stared hard at the stage, then checked her phone once more, before turning away from Heidi.

'Wait,' Heidi said.

'You have to talk to us,' Lucie broke in. 'A life depends on it.'

Still, the woman ignored them, circling in the opposite direction, smiling and laughing and joining in conversations. The room was buzzing again now. Bodie saw only one way of dealing with this.

Surround her.

There were enough of them. They formed a tight loop around Paulina to stop her from moving.

'Please,' Bodie began. 'Just five minutes.'

Paulina looked over their heads, craning her neck. Would she make a scene here, now, just to ward them off?

'Help us,' Yasmine said.

And then Paulina met their eyes. She looked from one to the other with hatred. 'Can't you see I'm busy? You're in the way.'

'We need your help.'

'I'm busy. Go away.'

'Manny LaRoy,' Bodie said. 'Your brother. Your family. He wants something from you and won't stop until he gets it. Best to get it out of the way now.'

Paulina checked her phone, scrolled through her recent posts. It was probably about time for another selfie. 'The world of the fashionista never stops,' she said. 'Five minutes with you could cost me dearly in the high visibility stakes. I just don't have the time.'

'You could save a life,' Heidi reiterated.

'One life is nothing to me. I am in charge of my destiny.'

Bodie couldn't plumb the depths of her self-centredness. There would be no getting through to her, he knew. 'All you have to do is listen,' he tried. 'And then answer. That's it.'

'I doubt I can spare a moment for you.'

'The LaRoy family Stanza,' Bodie went on. 'We need your line.'

This made her eyes narrow, her face go hard. Just for a moment. After that, it returned to its happy, serene expression, and she was craning to look around them once again.

'Please go away,' she said.

Bodie despaired. They had done well so far, extracted three lines of the stanza from LaRoy's siblings. This time, they weren't going to be so lucky.

The woman tried to squeeze through them. Reilly closed the gap, but they couldn't continue like this. They tried again, pleading for help, for just a line of the stanza in return, but the woman was too full of herself.

'I don't want to scream for help,' she said sweetly. 'It might attract too much attention. But I will if I have to.'

'Too much attention,' Bodie said, shaking his head. 'Are you kidding? You won't-'

Paulina put a hand on her hips and faced him. 'Do you like the way I look?' she asked him.

'What?'

Paulina swayed her hips back and forth on the spot. 'I like the way I look.'

'We don't have time for your shenanigans now? We need to-'

Paulina thrust her hips at Bodie. 'I can make you want me.'

'For fuck's sake,' Heidi stepped forward.

But Paulina just changed direction towards Heidi instead. 'You too, lovely,' she said. 'I go all ways.'

Bodie was at a loss. Nothing could penetrate this woman's sense of herself, of the fact that everything revolved around her.

'We're not gonna get through to you, are we?' he asked.

'There are ways.' She still had a hand on her hips

and now held her phone out and pursed her lips, taking another selfie.

'What do you want from us?' Lucie tried a new tack.

It was then that the shadowy figure darted towards them.

CHAPTER TWENTY FOUR

Right there, in the middl
of the gala full of ritzy guests, Raffaele and his men attacked.

Bodie hadn't seen them approach. He'd been too focused on Paulina and her ridiculous shenanigans. That they now approached almost blew his mind.

Here?

Raffaele grabbed hold of Paulina's wrist and yanked her forward. He was accompanied by two men, different ones yet again. They all wore dark suits. One man had shoved Heidi in the back to get her out of the way.

People were staring. Bodie saw Paulina dragged towards the entrance and exit doors to the room.

'Hey!' he shouted.

There was a sudden, very loud commotion. People were staring now, their mouths falling open in shock. In the tumult, Raffaele had dragged Paulina very close to the exit of the room. Bodie yelled and followed. One of Raffaele's goons blocked his path. Bodie was about to confront him when Reilly stepped in, taking the man, leaving Bodie free to go after Paulina.

A security guard stood near the door. He saw Paulina being dragged towards him and stepped forward, yelling at Raffaele. There was a sudden flash, a spray of blood, and the security guard went down. Raffaele continued to pull Paulina along.

It occurred to Bodie now that, instead of finessing the name out of her, instead of asking, Raffaele and whoever controlled him had just kidnapped the woman. How they intended to do that from the Met was anyone's guess.

But Raffaele was succeeding.

Bodie broke out into a run. Behind him, he heard Reilly fighting with one of the goons, Yasmine with the other. He saw a shadow to his right and turned to see Heidi jogging there.

'This is absurd,' she said. 'How can he hope to succeed?'

'He is succeeding. Shock and awe.'

They ran faster, catching up now. Raffaele had pulled Paulina out of the door, the black-clad woman pulling against her captor but otherwise not knowing what to do. They were in the hall outside, their shoes clacking against the polished marble floor.

Back inside the room, Reilly had his opponent in a headlock. A young man with a tight shirt had come to help and was standing, looking as if he didn't quite know what to do. Other people were calling the cops. Some were shouting for security. The artist had been left on stage, a tall, forlorn figure.

Yasmine had confronted the second goon, kicked him in the stomach, and brought him to his knees. He'd struck out, catching her knee and making her wobble. The dress she wore wasn't exactly suited to kicking, but she did it again, this time striking him in the chest. He wobbled, his face twisted in a rictus of pain.

Outside the room, Bodie and Heidi finally caught up to Raffaele.

'Let go of her,' Bodie yelled, so that it was clear to those standing around what was happening.

'What are you doing?' Heidi cried out.

Paulina was waving her free hand now, trying to get attention, which wasn't exactly something new for her. She stomped her feet and launched into a tirade at Raffaele. She tried to pull away, but the killer was far too strong for her.

He dragged her across the Great Hall.

Bodie caught up. He ran in front of them, got in Rafaele's way.

'Let the lady go,' he said.

Paulina stopped her shouting. She looked at him. 'Please,' she said.

Raffaele snarled in Bodie's face. He didn't want to let go of Paulina, so raised just one hand. Bodie didn't move a muscle.

Heidi came up from behind. 'Just let her go,' she said.

Raffaele attacked, dragging Paulina with him. He lashed out at Bodie with a fist, the attack incredibly fast. It hit Bodie in the side of the head, sent him to one side. For a moment, he saw double.

Heidi tried to grab Raffaele's shirt, but he was too quick. Now, he scooted past them, broke out into a run. Paulina wailed at his side. As one, they raced across the hall. Bodie didn't let them get away, though. He shook his head to clear the pain and ran after. To left and right there were other men looking to get involved now, shaping up to chase after Raffaele.

That was when the killer drew his gun. He waved it in the air as he ran.

'Do not come near me,' he called out.

Bodie knew he wouldn't fire it unless he had to. It would attract too much unwanted attention. There might even be cops outside. What was his escape plan?

They ran for the doors. Bodie decided to go for broke. There was no other choice. He ran hard, sped up as fast as he could, and threw himself at Raffaele's back, hitting so hard both men went tumbling. For a moment, Paulina was free. She froze on the spot, staring at the tumbling men.

'Run!' Heidi yelled.

Paulina didn't move.

Bodie grabbed Raffaele's gun wrist, held it tight. The weapon wavered in his general direction. A shot went off. The bullet slammed across the floor, smashing into a cabinet on the far side. Bodie tried to climb onto Raffaele's back.

When the gun went off, Paulina screamed. Still, she didn't move. Heidi could see her right hand flexing around her phone. She was still hanging on to it as though it were a lifeline. Heidi put a hand on the woman's shoulders.

She flinched, whipped her head around towards Heidi.

'Run,' she said. 'Hide. They're here for the line too.'

Paulina gaped at her, then switched her gaze to the fallen, struggling Raffaele. She looked too terrified to move.

Bodie kicked out at Raffaele's head. The killer weaved back and forth, avoiding the attacks. Bodie kept hold of the gun hand, tried to manoeuvre himself into a better position.

Just then, Yasmine, Jemma, Reilly and Lucie came running into the hall. They were wild-eyed, looking for their friends.

Bodie needed help. His grip was loosening on Raffaele's wrist.

They pounded forward. Behind them, the goons

came, looking the worse for wear. They were bloodied and shambling, but they still kept coming and yelled out a warning to the running relic hunters.

'Do not get involved.'

There were moments of wild chaos. The goons lumbering along. Reilly and his cohorts sprinting just in front. Bodie and Raffaele gripped in the deepest tension on the floor. Heidi and Paulina were stuck in stasis, unsure what to do next.

Raffaele yanked his gun arm away from Bodie, dropping the weapon in the process. He shot to his feet, kicked out, but Bodie blocked it and then pivoted from his knees to his feet. Both men faced each other.

Raffaele lunged at Paulina. Heidi got in the way, warding him off. Behind them, the goons threw themselves at Reilly and Yasmine, sending them sprawling, then rolled and tried to race to Raffaele's aid. This time Jemma and Lucie stepped in, holding them up until Reilly and Yasmine could rise to their feet.

Bodie faced Raffaele.

'You're done,' he said.

They could hear sirens outside in the street.

Raffaele gritted his teeth, looked to his men, and beckoned them across. The two men disengaged from the fight and ran around the outside of the hall, heading for the large doors. Raffaele grunted at Bodie.

'You saved the bitch this time. But we'll be back.'

'Not here you won't.' Bodie stood over the gun and between Raffaele and Paulina. With a shrug of his shoulders, the killer started running for the exit, stripping off his jacket so that all he wore was a white shirt. The goons did the same and disappeared through the entrance doors.

Bodie heaved a sigh of relief. Clearly, Raffaele had an escape route. He couldn't hope the cops would catch the killer out there, especially when they still thought the fight was in here. Bodie heaved a sigh of relief and kicked the gun away. He didn't want to remain near it.

'You saved me,' Paulina said softly. 'I didn't ask you to.'

'But we did it anyway,' he said a bit harshly.

'I am worth saving,' Paulina said. 'Me. You know, me.'

'Yes, we know who you are.'

'He had me. He was trying to rip me from this life. My life. But you saved me.'

Bodie eyed her. He had the distinct sense she was trying to say something, but had forgotten how to go about it.

'Is that an apology? Or a thank you?' Heidi asked.

'Well, I live my life for myself. I don't ask for help. I'm powerful enough, loved, revered. I have fans.'

'I would stay out of the limelight for a while,' Bodie said. 'Raffaele isn't done with you. Get some security.'

Paulina looked at him with an expression of thanks. By now, cops were rushing through the outer doors, looking around. Bodie waved at them.

'I have line two of the Stanza,' Paulina said lightly. '*A Gemstone Covered Cavern*. It isn't much, but it's all I have to give you.'

Bodie heaved a great sigh. 'Thank you.'

'Just think of me,' Paulina said as the cops approached. 'Think of me always.'

CHAPTER TWENTY FIVE

LaRoy was going crazy.

A few days had passed since he'd abducted Cassidy Coleman and sent Guy Bodie and his cohorts on their merry quest. They were long days, days in which the frustration, the anxiety, the fear, the worry of what might happen and what inevitably would happen, all ate him, gnawing away in his gut, muddling his head. He couldn't think straight, couldn't think about a single subject for more than a few minutes at a time. What was Bodie doing? Would his bastard siblings give up their lines? How could he hurt Cassidy enough to send her back broken to Bodie? How long would it all take?

Seconds passed into minutes and hours, each one making slow progress as if it was crawling through tar.

LaRoy tried to busy himself with work. There was plenty to do. But, again, he just couldn't concentrate and he had plenty of subordinates to take up the slack. There was all this worry in him, roiling so solid and large that he couldn't shake it even for a minute.

He sat now at his desk inside the big house on the estate. It was a lovely sunny morning and, outside, the tops of the trees were awash with gold, practically on fire, but he saw none of it. His eyes were fixed inward, evaluating. He sipped coffee, wishing it was later so that he could sip something stronger. Already this morning he'd tried to complete two work tasks and had made mistakes both times.

It wasn't worth it.

He might as well concentrate on that which bothered him the most. On Bodie. There were seven lines of the stanza. Obviously, they had his own, and by now, he hoped they would have four others. Last night was the gala. Bodie and his team should have met up with Paulina. LaRoy grinned without humour. He imagined that would have been an interesting meeting.

But the lines of stanza were stacking up, which was both a happy and fearful prospect. Something Bodie had said had taken root in his mind. What if, after all this, his father had been playing them? It was a dreadful thought, but that didn't stop it grinding at him. The old man would get the greatest kick from something like that.

LaRoy looked further inward. Life had never been free and happy and straightforward. There had always been a noose around his neck in the shape of his father. Memories were unwelcome and intrusive, and there were so many of them. Even thoughts of his siblings were better than thoughts of his father.

LaRoy rose, walked around the room. It was plushly laid out with polished fittings, a pendant chandelier, and a lavishly appointed desk. There were a couple of formal chairs arrayed before the desk and a leather couch in the far corner. LaRoy walked for a while, unable to get through a minute without experiencing some form of anxiety.

There was another problem, too. A tremendous problem.

Someone in his own organisation was betraying him.

They were sending men to the same places as Bodie, trying to wring the lines of the stanza from his siblings but in a far more violent manner. LaRoy wasn't above violence, obviously, but these men were killing innocents who got in the way, leaving a trail of bodies behind them.

LaRoy had been watching the news bulletins. Wherever Bodie went, there were reports of killings or nasty disturbances. Always something. It all helped cement the fact that someone else was after the lines of the stanza. They wanted the gemstones too.

LaRoy was careful to keep the information between a chosen few. He had no option to share details of the operation with them. He needed their input, their expertise, their logistical skills. The three men he shared information with were Friday, his second-in-command, Hirsch and Braun.

One of these three men was a traitor.

LaRoy wanted to narrow it down to one, of course. But he currently wasn't in the right headspace. His brain felt like it was crawling with fire ants. There was some kind of pressure at the front of his head, something weighing him down.

He couldn't think straight.

To distract himself, he picked up a phone and hit speed dial. The man who answered almost immediately was Friday, his second-in-command. The man he most trusted.

'Any luck with Hirsch and Braun?' he asked.

'Nothing so far, sir. They both seem pretty clean.'

'Then that leaves you, Friday.'

The man laughed. 'This must be handled delicately. We're digging into their past, their lives. The computer tech I'm using is treading lightly, looking for a money or information trail. It takes time when you do it right.'

'Follow the money,' LaRoy said.

'That's the idea, but, as I said, we have to do it with a light touch.'

LaRoy breathed in deeply and then let out an explosive breath. He hated light touch. He wanted to come down hard on someone.

Speaking of that...

'And how is our guest this morning?'

'Complaining. Angry. Sarcastic. Hard to handle. I'll be glad when she's gone.'

'Well, yes, because then we'll have accomplished our goal. And, speaking of that, I haven't heard from Bodie about his latest exploit yet. I wonder if he needs a small prompt.'

'A prompt?'

LaRoy had an idea that might help assuage the pressure in his head. A minor diversion. Yes, that would help.

'I'll be down shortly.'

'Here? To see Cassidy?'

'Yes. Make sure she can't attack me.'

LaRoy stood up, already warming to his task. He felt a little better already, but the gnawing was still there, right at the front of his head. He left the room, locked it after him, and made his way down an oak-panelled staircase to the ground floor. From there, he found the door that led to the basement and started down a long flight of concrete steps. The air smelled dank down here and it was cooler. There were other smells too, age and mould and sweat. Dust was everywhere, laid on every surface and spinning in the air. Spotlights had been attached to the ceiling and bathed the place in a stark, white light. LaRoy passed two guards, who nodded amiably. They carried guns in shoulder holsters and had Tasers attached to their waists. These guys wouldn't mess around if Cassidy tried to escape, but they had been ordered not to kill her outright.

LaRoy saw Friday ahead and raised a hand. The man came to meet him.

'She's cuffed.'

'Good. She'll need to be.'

'Boss?'

'I want to send Bodie a message. A hard one. Get your phone out.'

Friday nodded, frowning, and then let out a deep breath. He wasn't sure such an action was needed, obviously, but then he didn't call the shots. LaRoy did. And LaRoy wanted the fretful pressure in his head to go away.

He walked to the cell door. It was thick wood with bars acting as a vision panel at head height. He gripped the bars and stared through.

Cassidy was sitting on a narrow camp bed, her red hair falling across her shoulders. She was holding a plastic cup of water in her cuffed hands and sipping it slowly. No other furniture adorned the room, it was simply four cinder block walls. As LaRoy stood there, Cassidy looked up.

'Asshole,' she said by way of greeting.

LaRoy concentrated on her. 'I hope you're well.'

'I will be as soon as you get me out of here. Is that why you've come? To let me go.'

'Not exactly,' LaRoy turned and beckoned one guard forward.

'Taze her,' he said. 'Make it hurt.'

He lifted the phone, pressed the video icon and started recording. The guard came over, went through the doors of the cell, and approached Cassidy. LaRoy found he was grinning, the pressure eased for now. He focused in on Cassidy's body and then her face and then panned to the guard.

'Do it.'

The guard moved in warily, unhappily. He didn't want to get too close to the woman, you could tell. But he touched the Taser to the bars and let it fizzle, then the camp bed. Cassidy didn't flinch once, just stared at him.

The guard reached out for her. Cassidy finally reacted, standing and lashing out but, before her attack could land, the long handled Taser touched her. It made her fold, made her cry out. The cup of water flew to the side. Cassidy hit the camp bed on her side.

The guard warmed to his task, hitting her again and again. Every touch made her flinch and cry out, but she stayed as still as possible, fully aware there was no way out for her. The guard made sure not to touch anything vital. He seemed to enjoy focusing on the ribs.

LaRoy filmed every second. It was a shame he couldn't get Cassidy's face in the shot, but that would be too risky. Twice already, Cassidy had lashed out at the guard, barely missing him. The guy was lucky he could stand so far away and still employ the juice.

The guard paused, looked over at LaRoy. 'That enough?'

'Give her a couple more, just for fun.'

The phone would pick his voice up. Bodie would hear all of it. LaRoy grinned behind the device, focusing in gleefully when the Taser touched the woman. Her grunts were weakening a little. She was clearly exhausted by the pain. LaRoy liked that too.

'I think we should stop now, sir,' Friday said at his side. 'We don't want to kill her.'

'A few more, I think.'

'She's the only leverage we have over Bodie.'

LaRoy grimaced. His second-in-command was right.

If Cassidy expired, they had no hold over Bodie. He bit his lip.

'How'd you like that, Bodie?' he whispered into the phone. 'You'd better be making progress, my friend. Cassidy will get this treatment every day.'

He nodded at the guard, ordering him to back away. Cassidy didn't move, just lay staring at the wall, chest heaving. LaRoy ended the video and chuckled.

'Well, that was fun!' he shouted at Cassidy. 'Same time tomorrow?'

She didn't answer. LaRoy didn't really blame her. He handed the phone to Friday.

'Get that to Bodie immediately,' he said. 'I don't want him thinking he has any kind of hold over us. Show him who's really in charge.'

'Yes, sir.'

LaRoy looked away from Cassidy. He was pleased. A very distracting few minutes had passed, and he felt much better. Maybe torturing people was the way forward. That was something to think about, at least.

He put his mind to thinking of something more elaborate for Cassidy.

CHAPTER TWENTY SIX

Bodie had a nasty premonition when the video file came in. He knew it could be nothing good.

They sat in the hotel lobby, planning their next moves. Bodie was feeling gutted. They'd spent some time laying out the lines of the stanza and analysing them.

'A Ghost Town famous in the nineteenth century,
A Gemstone Covered Cavern,
The Eighteen Million Dollar Goldmine,
Where Presidents and Generals tarry, drinking champagne,
I see diamonds, gold, the richest gemstones.'

'It offers us nothing,' Lucie had said. 'No clues. No locations. Just five generic lines.'

'Then the last two must be revealing,' Reilly said. 'Assuming we can get them.'

'We *have* to get them,' Bodie said.

'Is there an eighteen million dollar goldmine where presidents and generals sipped champagne? Have you checked?' Heidi asked.

'I'm sure there is,' Lucie spread her hands. 'But it's too vague. It encompasses every old goldmine in America. People like the president and generals visited a lot of them.'

Reilly leaned forward. 'I know I'm the new guy here,' he said. 'I know I'm fresh from the Amazon and potentially still being hunted. But can't we draft in a little help?'

Lucie stared at him. 'We don't need help,' she said. 'If we can't figure it out, the information simply isn't there. We've been doing this a while now.'

Yasmine put a hand on Reilly's shoulder, pressing hard. Bodie was reminded that they were once a couple and might be interested in starting up where they left off. It was none of his business, so he left it alone. He thought Reilly, tagging along with them, wasn't a bad thing. The guy was bloody useful.

But he came with baggage. Behind his electric blue eyes was a history with the Bratva, a betrayal, and a certainty that they would try to make him pay. Maybe they had forgotten about him by now... maybe not.

Bodie smiled at the man. 'We take some getting used to,' he said. 'But we do know what we're doing.'

Reilly nodded and sat back, ran a hand through his shock of long, blonde hair. 'I trust you,' he said.

It was actually a big compliment, coming from the man who'd led them one step at a time through the Amazon jungle, who they had relied on to keep them alive. Bodie nodded in thanks.

Just then, his phone buzzed.

He looked down. 'Crap,' he said.

'What is it?' Heidi asked as Jemma leaned forward.

'Not good. It's a video file, and it's from an unknown number.'

He pulled up the file and clicked on the link. Then he played it. What he saw made him close his eyes and his blood run cold. Silently, he watched it twice and then handed it around his circle of colleagues.

'Ah, shit,' Heidi said. 'That's horrible.'

The others expressed similar statements and shock.

Cassidy's video was accompanied by a simple message. *Get a move on.*

Bodie had been waiting until they'd decided on something to make the call to LaRoy.

Now, he said it aloud. 'Leverage.'

They all nodded. Heidi picked up a coffee and drank two swallows before saying, 'He's gonna kill her at the end of all this. Maybe try to kill us too. We can't put ourselves into that situation.'

'Agreed,' Bodie said. 'But the bastard has us on a short leash, as evidenced by that video. We tried to drag it out, to give us some breathing space in which to work, and look what happens.'

'We have gained a lot of time though,' Jemma pointed out. 'Usually, we call LaRoy right after the job. Now, it's the next morning.'

'It will give us some free time if we get him used to it,' Reilly said.

'Time to do what, though?' Bodie asked.

'It would be easier if we didn't have the other enemy on our asses,' Heidi said.

Bodie nodded. 'We don't even know who they are,' he said. 'Shit, *LaRoy* doesn't even know who they are. But they keep turning up like bad eggs.'

'We can press LaRoy for the information,' Bodie said. 'And use it to keep him slightly in the dark. That could be our excuse for not calling right away.'

The others agreed. Bodie put his phone on the table, face down, as if that could somehow ward off the images of seeing Cass tortured. He needed to call LaRoy, but he couldn't bring himself to do it straight away.

'There is only one form of leverage that I can think of,' Lucie said.

Bodie already knew what she would say. He looked up at her. 'Yes?'

'The gemstones,'

'You're saying that, in just a few hours, after we get the last clue, that we *find* the missing gemstones, track them down, and then steal them, hold them to ransom?' Jemma said.

They were all thinking the same thing.

'To be fair,' Bodie said. 'It's kind of what we do.'

'Obviously it depends on the location of the mine,' Reilly said. 'But there will be a period of stasis. We can drag it out before telling LaRoy the last line, and then we can keep moving as he gears up to go to the mine. There could be time.'

'It's our only chance,' Jemma said forlornly.

'Cassidy for the gemstones,' Bodie said. 'It would work.'

There were several nods of agreement from around the table. It felt better to know they had a plan, that they weren't just chasing their tails at LaRoy's beck and call. He now clenched his fists, swallowed, and geed himself up to make an unwanted, despised call.

'LaRoy,' he said when the phone was answered.

'Ah, Bodie, you rang. Finally.'

'We've been under pressure from these other goons who are after the stanza lines. You have any clue who's the rat in your organisation yet?'

LaRoy was silent for a long moment. 'We are still rooting it out. Do not let it interfere with your own task.'

Bodie fought hard not to show his anger. 'We face the fallout every day,' he said. 'These people are trying to kill us, too.'

'Boohoo. Now, did Paulina give you her line?'

LaRoy sounded as if he was bursting with excitement.

Bodie put the pressure on. It was petty, but it was his minor victory. 'She turned out to be the hardest nut to crack so far.'

'I told you she was a complex one.'

For once, Bodie agreed with LaRoy. Paulina had been all kinds of complicated.

'She wouldn't hear anything that wasn't about herself,' he dragged it out.

'Yes, yes, I know, but did you get the line?'

Bodie couldn't think of anything else, so relented. 'Yes, you fucker, we got the line. But if you want us to keep helping you, you will leave Cassidy alone from now on.'

There was a silence, and then LaRoy chuckled. 'She did squirm, didn't she?'

'You are an utter freak.'

'Thank you. I do try. I told you on the video that Cassidy will experience the same treatment every day.'

'You can't do that to a precious prisoner,' he knew it was useless but had to try.

'Consider yourself lucky if she comes back in one piece.'

Bodie bit his tongue to calm himself. 'We're doing everything you asked. We now have five lines of the stanza. Do you want to hear Paulina's?'

'Yes,' LaRoy said eagerly.

'*A Gemstone Covered Cavern.*'

LaRoy didn't reply at first, as if expecting more. Then, he said, 'Is that it?'

'That's it.'

'We might as well not have bothered. All that work for a crappy line.'

'And that only leaves two lines,' Bodie reminded him.

'I'm well aware of that.'

Bodie knew that they, the relic hunters, were in real trouble. LaRoy owned them and could make them jump through any hoop. Still, he tried to maintain the upper hand. 'Are you sure your father hasn't fucked you, LaRoy?'

'It can't be. I refuse to believe it.'

'Are you sure the damn gemstones are real?' It was a question they really needed an answer to for their own plan.

'Yes, yes, they're real. I've seen them. Father made sure we all saw them before telling us what he'd done. The location of the mine will be genuine.'

'And Cass will be released when you get the location, not when you find the stones?'

'That is the deal.'

'So tell me,' Bodie said. 'All about the next fucked-up sibling of yours.'

CHAPTER TWENTY SEVEN

Cassidy lay on her camp bed, clutching her ribs. Pain still filled her head, a ghost pain that made her limbs shiver.

She stretched, forced herself to move. The punishment she'd taken had been extreme; she could tell the guard and LaRoy enjoyed inflicting it. They'd gone on far too long until she had almost lost control. Cassidy was a hardened street fighter, a tough nut. A hard life had taught her hard ways, and now she was having to draw on all her reserves just to survive one more day.

One more night.

She wouldn't break. She could tell that was what LaRoy wanted. He desired to see a blubbering wreck, someone who would beg for mercy. He wanted her shivering and pleading and terrified.

Well, she wouldn't comply.

Cassidy sat up, pulled her knees up to her chest. The camp bed creaked. She looked out through her bars, saw a guard leering in at her. The door was locked. Lucky for him. She looked away, stared at the concrete walls. It had been a long few days.

LaRoy had now told her roughly what was happening. He had tasked Bodie and the others with a quest, something about recovering a load of expensive gemstones. LaRoy needed them for some reason that he wouldn't reveal.

Cassidy felt the pain begin to subside. She moved gingerly, rubbed her ribs. The bastard guard had also zapped her in the backs of her thighs, and the muscles there were involuntarily spasming. She rubbed them too, wanting the sensation to go away.

She turned her attention elsewhere.

She was figuring a way out. There was no give in the concrete walls, no gaps and, besides, the guards looked in on her regularly and randomly. Her only way out was through the front door of her cage.

To that end, Cassidy was working on something. They brought her food three times a day. Three different men visited her randomly, placing the plates and cups on the floor and then backing out. Two of the men were brutes, staring at her, watching her, but the third man was a little softer. He smiled at her, gave her sad eyes, as if he was sorry she was locked up. He appeared to sympathise with her plight.

She started talking to him.

He was young, early twenties, and she'd found out that his name was Arthur. Arthur was a gamer; he loved all types of PlayStation games and, once work was done for the day, could always be found sprawled out with a controller in his hand. He loved to immerse himself in those new worlds, probably because he hated his own.

Arthur might be young, but he carried the weight of the world with him. His face was lined; he looked in his thirties and he walked with a bowed back. He always had a smile for her, though.

'You don't enjoy this life,' she said once.

'I hate it,' he confided softly. 'I'd do anything to get out.'

'Then help me.' Right then, another guard had

crossed to the door and told Arthur to get a move on. The young man had looked at her, an expression of enquiry on his face, and had then backed away.

Every time since then, Arthur had brought and removed the food and plates. The conversations had turned, and she'd garnered information about Bodie and the rest of the relic hunters.

Now she knew exactly why she'd been kidnapped.

Arthur explained all about the gemstones and the lost mine where they'd been buried. He told her about LaRoy's father and the fiendish stanza he'd left behind to taunt his sons and daughters. Cassidy had laid a hand on the man's shoulder, thanking him. He had reacted as she'd hoped, with a smile. He told her about Bodie's exploits, about the team's visit to the sanitorium and the middle of nowhere, and revealed the rumour that someone else was busy searching for the gemstones too. Arthur was a font of information, a goldmine himself.

'Any idea who the traitor is?' Cassidy had asked, knowing the men would talk among themselves.

Arthur had shaken his head. 'Could be anyone. But it has to be someone close to LaRoy.'

Cassidy toyed briefly with the idea of joining forces with that person, but then realised even if she could find out who it was through Arthur, the chances of him helping her out were remote. She could only hope that the traitor was disrupting LaRoy's plans, because that would help keep her alive longer.

On that front, she was certain LaRoy intended to kill her.

Nothing had been said, but the guy was clearly a killer. He loved inflicting pain. He liked to watch. If he succeeded in his quest, there would be no reason to keep her alive. And this was a very large estate. Things – anything – could vanish without trace... forever.

Which, again, made her relationship with Arthur even more important.

Cassidy had to find a way out of here. She started walking around the cell, keeping her limbs moving, trying to ward any lethargy away. Her ribs ached, her thighs too. She walked anyway, grimacing through the pain.

She wondered how many guards there were. She'd been keeping count and, so far, had seen seven different faces. And that was just down here. But there were only two at a time. That wasn't a terrible number if she could overpower one of them.

But the rest of the house? That was an unknown. She'd mentioned it to Arthur, but she wasn't completely past his defences yet. He wasn't sure he wanted to throw his lot in with her. Arthur had reddened slightly and then changed the subject, talking breezily about *Fifa 23* and *Sonic Racing* and *Minecraft*. Cassidy let him go on for a bit, knowing the other guard could hear him talking loudly. It was an excellent cover for their clandestine chats.

Another question that plagued her: could she make a weapon?

The guards carried Tasers but not guns. At least, not the ones she'd had guarding her down here. They fed her on paper plates and gave her plastic cups. Utensils were plastic forks and knives, and they always took those away. Her camp bed was made of tubular steel though, and some bolts were loose. She fancied she might be able to unscrew one of the uprights to use as a weapon.

LaRoy was making her life harder, coming into her

cell each morning to watch the guards tase her. It seemed to be the highlight of his day. He couldn't get enough of her pain. Once it was over, he turned on his heel and bounced away with a sprightly step, whistling to himself. Even the guards exchanged wondering looks behind his back.

It all came down to one thing.

Cassidy simply had to find a way out of here.

She checked the bolts of her camp bed for the hundredth time, made sure they were as loose as possible. She went through what she needed to ask Arthur in her head. Questions about the guards and their shift changes, about how many were stationed up top, about the estate she was in and how close it was to New York. Did he have access to a car? Would he even help her escape?

Decision time was looming.

As far as Cassidy knew, Bodie and the team were closing in on the gemstones. They didn't have many more siblings to go.

Cassidy had to be ready to act.

HIERARCHY OF MADNESS

CHAPTER TWENTY EIGHT

Bodie listened hard as LaRoy explained everything he knew about the fifth family member they would have to visit.

'Stuart LaRoy,' Cassidy's abductor rolled the name around his tongue. 'A real piece of work.'

Bodie almost rolled his eyes. 'Tell us all about him.'

They were still seated in the lobby, gathered around Bodie and the phone and listening to LaRoy. The morning was passing quietly, and they were getting some much needed rest. But, as soon as the phone had rung, Bodie had snatched it up.

LaRoy spoke again, but Bodie interrupted. 'And stop hurting Cassidy,' he said. 'We're playing your games. There's no need.'

'But it gets me through the day.'

'You'll get your comeuppance, LaRoy.'

'But not today. Now, are you ready to listen?'

Bodie said nothing.

'Stuart LaRoy is known, at least to me, as the Collector. He's obsessive, zealous, addicted. Everything in his home is kept under lock and key. I guess you could call him a hermit. Stuart rarely leaves home and, even then, it's only to collect some new item or other. Stuart hates people. He's paranoid to the extreme-'

'You people make me sick,' Heidi interrupted with a deep sigh.

LaRoy ignored her. 'Stuart hates other people so much that, if they come near him, he threatens to kill them.'

'So he's gonna be a challenge,' Bodie said sarcastically.

'He's certainly not a talker. Stuart has a few convictions and minor complaints against him, but he asserts he has a right to defend his property. He has been known to shoot at cars that have gone down the wrong driveway or parked too closely outside his house.'

'How the hell do you expect us to get the man's line?' Jemma asked.

'Your problem, I'm afraid, but Cassidy will thank you for it.'

'I want to speak to her,' Bodie said.

'You're not speaking with her. She's fine, for the most part. We're looking after her, keeping her warm and comfortable.'

'What's that supposed to mean?'

'Nothing. You're getting off track. Stuart's vast home is a museum. He has several alarms and cameras and lives alone, of course. He's practically impossible to get close to. The man drives people off all the time, not allowing them to get near. You will have your work cut out, I'm afraid.' LaRoy almost sounded sorry for them.

Almost.

'Where does he live?' Yasmine asked.

LaRoy gave them an address in northern New York state several hours' drive away. Bodie calculated the journey in his mind. 'Anything else?' he asked.

'Should there be? Just get me that fucking line.'

'How about an update on the assholes who keep turning up?'

HIERARCHY OF MADNESS

'Oh, that. I'm close to uncovering the culprit, don't worry.'

'So, are they gonna be there again? This Raffaele and his goons?' Reilly's question.

'I'd keep an eye out for them.'

Bodie hissed at LaRoy's sarcasm. For a man relying on them, he wasn't much help. He jabbed at the phone, ending the call, and then looked around the table.

'Mount up,' he said.

They didn't waste any time. The team jumped in their car, programmed the sat nav, and set off. As Reilly drove, the others tried to decide what to do about Stuart LaRoy.

'I'm torn,' Yasmine said. 'I don't want to threaten, intimidate or hurt the guy, but how else are we even gonna get near him?'

'He has no problem doing that to others,' Heidi reminded them.

The car hummed through the midmorning traffic, snarled up for a while at first and then easing off. Rows of houses and eating establishments and small shops passed on both sides, windows open to admit the warm day, people sitting outside and enjoying the sun. Bodie and the others drove through a land of peace and quiet and indifference, lost in their turmoil. Bodie's stomach twisted with every passing second, his emotions churned up. He wasn't hungry, could barely concentrate. All his worry was for Cass, and for what might be happening to her even now as they tried to find LaRoy's next sibling.

There were only two lines of the stanza left.

It gnawed hard at Bodie. He was normally an

optimist, a proactive man who always strived to keep moving forward. Today, though, and recently, he had found himself being bogged down with indecision, with errant thoughts, and all of it centred on the loss of Cassidy. As he sat there, as he talked, as he thought, he worried about her.

'We do what we're good at,' Jemma said. 'We infiltrate. I say we sneak into Stuart's house, find him, and confront him. I don't see any other way.'

They weren't just good at it, Bodie knew, they were exceptional.

'A proper old school infiltration,' he said.

'And a fast one,' Jemma said. 'Has to be tonight.'

Bodie agreed. Every moment they wasted cost Cassidy more pain. They weren't exactly geared up for an infiltration, but they could certainly make the best of it. 'I guess we wait and see what Stuart's house looks like,' he said. 'Access points. Infil points. The lot.'

Reilly, at the wheel, looked a little uncomfortable. 'We're breaking in?' he asked.

It reminded Bodie that Reilly was new to their team. He didn't really know how they operated yet, and he knew very little of their past.

'Difficult one, mate. Before we met you, we operated as relic hunters. That was a profession imposed on us by the CIA. They broke me out of a Mexican prison, forced us to take on a few extreme jobs. There was the statue of Zeus, Atlantis, the Amber Room, and more.'

'Atlantis? That was you?'

'Yes, and more. But that's not the point. We got out from under the thumb of the CIA eventually and now we're our own bosses.'

'So what are you now?'

'Well, that's just it, you see. We don't *know* what we

are now. We're between jobs, falling through the cracks. But the important thing for you to know is that we had a life before we became relic hunters.'

'Which brought you to the attention of the CIA?'

'Kind of. We were thieves, but only in the broadest sense of the word. We used to take on jobs that enabled us to steal from the bad guys, take their possessions, their technologies, sometimes help save the world. Basically, we got good at our job, one of the best teams in the world. We were always busy.'

'I didn't know that.' Reilly cast a glance back at Yasmine.

'I wasn't with them then either,' she said. 'I'm a baby on this team.'

Bodie was again reminded of Cassidy. She'd been with them all along, always by his side. He looked at Reilly.

'You comfortable with that?'

'Do I have a choice?'

'You don't have to come in with us.'

Reilly slowed to let a car come out of the inside lane. 'Sure. But I'm part of the team. At least I like to think I am.'

Bodie thought about that. He hadn't yet considered Reilly to be part of the team. In truth, he hadn't even been sure Reilly wanted to stay with them, kept wondering if the man might leave at any minute. Keeping Reilly with them added to their overall sense of peril. They'd already placated the Bratva once, years ago, and might have to do so again if they came calling for Reilly.

'You are a part of this team,' Yasmine said quickly.

Bodie was a little more standoffish. 'Is that what you want?' he asked, surprise in his voice.

'Good question,' Reilly said, squinting into the glare of sunlight off the road. 'I came with you all the way from the Amazon, helped you out there, fought and almost died with you. I've done the same since Cassidy got kidnapped. Despite all that, or maybe because of it, I still want to stay with you guys.'

Bodie considered it all. He looked back at Jemma. Oddly, he thought, Jemma was the only other person in the car left from the old days.

'I didn't realise,' he said aloud sadly.

It came as quite a shock. They had lost colleagues along the way. But Reilly was capable, intelligent, and useful.

'Welcome to the team,' he said. 'But you still don't have to come in with us tonight.'

Reilly nodded. 'I wouldn't miss it,' he said.

CHAPTER TWENTY NINE

Darkness coated the land as if some invisible giant had swiped a black-tarred brush from one side of the sky to the other. It was pure blackness, not a star or cloud in the sky, not even the faintest slither of a moon.

Bodie, in the car, nodded gratefully. 'This is good.'

They had found Stuart's house in the late afternoon, cruised by a couple of times and then found a place to park. One by one, they had exited and started strolling around his neighbourhood. Stuart lived in a quiet, leafy lane with cars parked on both sides of the street, with uncut grassy verges and refuse bins standing out at the kerb. It was a slice of suburbia that Bodie wasn't used to.

Stuart's house stood at the end of the lane and was larger than those around it. It was two-storey, masked by trees, and had black iron railings placed all the way around the garden. The railings were spiked, the black gate padlocked. The team made a full reconnoitre of the area, sneaking through the neighbouring gardens at one point, seeking an infiltration point into Stuart's house. They saw the CCTV, the yard floodlights, the closed drapes. They stayed low, out of sight, not wanting Stuart to see them lurking. It took time; they walked slowly and steadily, but eventually they had met up back at the car.

And hatched a plan.

It was pure dark now. Perfect. Bodie and the others were all dressed in black – more purchases that dwindled their funds – and had smeared blackout on their faces. They had rucksacks with tools and other items they might need. They stalked down the leafy neighbourhood, stealing through the gardens and from bush to bush until Stuart's imposing black railings stood in front of them.

Bodie reached out and started climbing.

He hadn't done this for a while. It actually felt odd and a little unsafe. He wasn't used to it. One day, years ago, it had been his life. Bodie climbed like a monkey, nipped over the spikes, and then jumped down into the garden on the other side. He crouched, waiting as the others did the same. The night was silent and still. His breath fogged from his mouth. He stayed low and alert, scanning from side to side. He could smell overturned earth and the fragrance of a nearby bed of flowers. From somewhere far away, a dog barked, briefly unsettling the night.

Bodie took a step towards the house and then another. Soon, he was standing with his back to the wall, the rough brick under his fingers. There was a metallic taste in his dry mouth and he knew it wasn't just nerves for Cassidy. It was related to this mission.

He moved to the door, a white PVC affair, and peered through the glass. Yes, he could see the key on the other side of the lock and the alarm panel next to the door. Some people preferred to leave their keys in the lock because it helped to prevent theft, but it could also aid a thief.

Bodie proceeded in silence. He took out a heavy glass cutter, cut out a hole in the vision panel, and used a rubber suction pad to pull the glass out. Carefully, he laid it on the ground. Now Jemma took over, being the consummate cat burglar. She reached into the house, unlocked the door, and let it open.

Immediately, an alarm began beeping.

This was the tricky part. Jemma had fashioned a device that could connect to an alarm and leech out the code in a matter of seconds from items purchased at a local RadioShack. Jemma had done it many times before, fine tuning her device through the years. Now she connected it to the alarm and watched the numbers flash up on the screen.

'Five. Nine. Seven. Six.'

She tapped it in. The alarm fell silent. It had been beeping softly for perhaps six seconds. If Stuart was asleep, which he hopefully would be at this time of night, he wouldn't have heard anything.

They were all inside, standing in Stuart's kitchen. A wooden table stood in front of them, surrounded by chairs, and the door was across the other side of the room. The kitchen was large and airy, with a central worktop area. Blinds cut any light that might have filtered in from outside.

Jemma led the way, as silent as a panther stalking its prey. She padded across the kitchen and through the door. Bodie followed, finding himself in a long hallway at the end of which stood a flight of stairs.

Of course, they expected to find LaRoy up those stairs. But they had to be careful because Stuart might even have fallen asleep on the sofa.

They swept the downstairs thoroughly, creeping from the kitchen to the dining room and then into the living room. They checked the conservatory, found that even that was curtained off. Bodie worried a little about Stuart's reaction. The man would probably try to kill them and they might have to go in hard. But Stuart was innocent, and he wasn't a naturally bad guy. It was just his madness that made him do what he did.

Everywhere, there were display cabinets, all full to bursting.

Bodie reached the bottom of the stairs and paused. He waited for the others to catch up, watched them in the dark. They were all breathing softly, making conservative movements. When they were ready, he started up, a riser at a time.

Only one step squeaked for him. The others avoided it. Bodie stopped still when it happened, listening intently, but again, nothing could be heard from above. He continued to the top of the stairs, using his torch sparingly.

Now he moved even more warily. In the gloom, he could see four doors along a passageway, all closed. The first was a bathroom, the others would all be bedrooms. The floor was carpeted and helped cushion their steps. Pictures hung on the walls, covering nearly every inch of space. As downstairs there were cabinets and display cases everywhere, all full. Bodie had never seen so much stuff collected in so small a place. The cabinets marched in two separate rows down the entire landing and, at the end where a window looked out, there stood a large bookcase full of memorabilia.

Bodie crept between it all. He reached the first bedroom. Slowly, he turned the handle, looked inside. It wasn't a bedroom at all – it was a storage room, cram packed with dusty bookcases, display cabinets and tables. Every inch of space had been taken up. Bodie backed out of the room.

Jemma took the second bedroom door, finding exactly the same scenario. The team checked anyway, just in case Stuart was sleeping on the floor or in a corner, but there was no sign of the man.

They approached the last room.

Bodie got there first, put his hand on the door handle. He took a deep breath, checked that the others were all ready. Then, he turned the door handle, and in silence, eased the door open.

Immediately, a terrible stench hit him. Something sickly crawled up from his stomach into his throat. Bodie closed his eyes briefly, then let the door open all the way.

This was Stuart's bedroom. There was a single bed in the centre, the now expected cabinets standing around all the walls. On the bed was Stuart, lying perfectly still, his arms by his side.

The reason for that was that Stuart was dead.

Blood pooled around the body, soaked into the sheets. Bodie put his hand over his nose and walked further into the bedroom.

Reilly passed him on the left, apparently oblivious to the stench. 'Throat cut,' he said, bending over the body.

'Recently?' Jemma asked.

'Damn it,' Bodie swore.

'Blood's pooled and sticky,' Reilly said. 'The sheets are all soaked through. I'd say this happened this afternoon sometime, maybe even before we got here.'

'Murder,' Bodie said. 'Raffaele arrived before us.'

'It sure seems that way,' Reilly said.

'Shit, now what the hell are we supposed to do?' Lucie asked.

The same question was in Bodie's mind. There was no way they were going to get Stuart's line of the stanza and it was one of the crucial ones, surely. It would be line six or seven. And now Raffaele possessed it.

He hadn't imagined things could get worse on their mission, but they certainly had.

'What do we do now?' Lucie repeated.

Bodie did not know. They had to continue on as normal. They had to hold off contacting LaRoy for as long as possible to get him used to the delay so that, when they located the gemstones, they could rush off and retrieve them. But LaRoy, when he found out, wouldn't like this. He would hit the roof.

And Cassidy would suffer.

'There's only one thing for it,' he said.

The others all looked at him. 'What?' Heidi asked.

'We go like hell for the last sibling.'

CHAPTER THIRTY

There was no choice but to call LaRoy urgently.

They raced out of the house in the dark, forced to stay stealthy so as not to alert any neighbours, picking their way through yards and along hedgerows. The car sat in the pitch black, waiting for them, and they piled in. Bodie's anxiety levels were through the roof. His stomach churned. All he could think of at first was how this would affect Cassidy.

Reilly started the car and drove off. They had never intended to stay anywhere tonight, so had no hotel room booked. Reilly pushed the car through the darkness.

Bodie, in the front seat, turned to the others.

'No choice,' he said.

It was the opposite of what they wanted to do, but Bodie plucked out his phone and dialled LaRoy's number. The phone was answered on the eighth ring.

'Hello?'

'Did I wake you, LaRoy? That's a shame.'

'Bodie? What the hell? Don't you know what time it is?'

'You wanted contacting immediately. So here we are. Next time, we'll wait.'

There was the sound of shuffling, of a pillow being rearranged and plumped. Then came the sound of someone drinking. After a while, LaRoy returned to the conversation.

'I'm ready for the line.'

Bodie felt his anxiety rise a notch. 'We were too late. Raffaele got there first.'

A sharp intake of breath. 'What?' LaRoy's voice was several octaves higher.

'We arrived, infiltrated the house, got all the way to the bedroom through the collections and found Stuart dead in bed. He'd been murdered.'

LaRoy let out a gruesome expletive. He sounded like he was punching something. It took a while for him to return to the phone.

'You've lost an entire line?'

Bodie sighed, but was glad Cassidy's name had not come up. 'Like I said, they beat us to it. All we can do now is get to the last sibling fast.'

'Fast? Yes, fast. Faster than this Raffaele character.'

'So I need information about the final sibling.'

'Of course. Just give me a minute.'

Bodie fixed his eyes dead ahead, seeing nothing through the windscreen. A minute later, a gas station popped up on the left and Reilly pulled in to top up the fuel tank. Everyone got out of the car after cleaning their faces and hands on towels and ended up buying provisions from a row of fridges that offered a welter of special deals. They bought pastries and sandwiches and drinks and then piled back into the car. Bodie sat waiting for LaRoy the entire time.

Soon, Reilly was back on the road.

LaRoy started speaking. Bodie turned on the speakerphone.

'My final, dear sibling is my sister, Anna. The Body Snatcher.'

LaRoy seemed to speak the last three words with a certain grim satisfaction.

Bodie made a face. 'The what?'

'You heard correctly. The Body Snatcher. Dear old Anna was once convicted of digging up bodies to experiment on. She's the oldest of us, a doctor. She ended up spending quite a few years in a wonderful upstate penitentiary but, since her release, hasn't been heard from much. I wonder why.'

Bodie shook his head in incredulity. 'Where are we headed?'

'New York. Queens. I'll send you the exact address.'

Reilly nodded in thanks, starting with tapping Queens into the sat nav.

Bodie took a breath. 'What else can you tell us about her?'

'She's a crazy old lady, old before her time, with wide eyes and long white hair. She will help anyone who gives her an interesting diversion.'

'What the hell is that supposed to mean?'

'How it sounds. You will have to come up with a promising digression. Something that really catches her attention.'

Bodie didn't know what to say. He wanted to ask LaRoy for ideas, for direction, but he knew the man would just laugh at him. Reilly put his foot down, barrelling through the night.

'This is your last chance, Bodie,' LaRoy said. 'Don't mess this one up.'

They drove as fast as they could, saw the approaching lights of New York with the sky still dark, and drove across the Manhattan Bridge as morning started firing up the eastern skies. A crimson glow split the darkness apart, burnishing the high rises of New York, reflecting off the windows. It was a surreal sight and it should have been a peaceful sight, but nobody in the car was calm. They were all on edge, all filled with roiling emotions.

They passed through Manhattan, a piece of Brooklyn, and then entered Queens. They were forced to stop for gas once more and made sure the car was filled to the brim. They ate and drank on the go, and had arrived outside Anna LaRoy's house by mid morning.

Reilly sat back, sighed, turned the car off. He gripped the wheel.

'See anything?' Heidi asked.

In the ticking silence, they studied the front of Anna's house.

'We shouldn't waste any more time,' Bodie said. 'We should go in.'

'Agreed,' Heidi said.

They exited the car quickly and walked across the road. The air was filled with the fumes of a passing car. Men and women strolled up and down the street, living their everyday lives, far removed from the hell in which the relic hunters walked. Bodie stopped in front of the house. It was a two-storey affair with drawn drapes, a fancy red front door and a wide step. Bodie walked up to the door and raised his hand to knock.

It opened instantly, the space suddenly filled with the head of a woman. Bodie stepped back in surprise.

'What do you want?' she snarled at him.

'Anna LaRoy?'

'What of it?'

The woman's face was deeply lined, her white hair hanging down both sides of her head. Her lower lip trembled and her eyes shone fiercely.

'We really need your help,' Bodie said.

'Do I look like I help dickheads who come to my step? Piss off.'

She moved to close the door. Bodie took a step towards her. 'You're in serious trouble,' he said.

She hesitated, hand on the door. 'What are you talking about?'

'Can we come in?' Heidi asked. 'Can we explain it to you? It's a long story.'

The woman's face screwed up so tightly that it resembled a craggy mountain range of ridges and clefts.

'Like I said, piss off. I don't need your help.'

'It involves Manny LaRoy,' Bodie said quickly. 'Your brother. And all your other siblings.'

The woman's face switched instantly, turning suspicious. 'Those bastards?'

All this time, Reilly and Yasmine had been watching the perimeter, staring out across the street in case Raffaele and his goons turned up.

Bodie went for it. 'Manny LaRoy has kidnapped our friend. He's making us find out the lines of the LaRoy family stanza, put them together, and then locate a mine. If we don't get it done, our friend dies.'

'He's looking for the gemstones.' the woman now looked interested.

'That's not all,' Heidi said. 'You're in danger too.' And she went on to explain about Raffaele and the traitor in Manny's organisation. Anna watched her for a long time after she finished speaking.

'Are you saying you want me out of my house?'

'As soon as possible,' Bodie struggled to hide his emotions.

'We can take you somewhere,' Jemma said. 'And talk.'

'Do you know who I am?'

It was an odd question, and it stopped Bodie on the spot. He squinted at her. 'What?'

'What I've done? The person I really am.'

Bodie nodded. 'Only what Manny told us. We know you went to prison in the past.'

'For what I did, they should have thrown away the key,' Anna said softly, almost to herself.

Bodie ignored that. He urged the woman to go with them, to leave what she thought was the safety of her house, but was in fact a deathtrap. He could understand her reluctance, but he needed her to come.

'Please,' he stressed.

It took another twenty minutes of cajoling with Reilly and Yasmine watching their backs, but they finally got Anna to accompany them to the lobby of a local hotel. As soon as the woman left the house, Bodie felt happier. They walked five blocks to a hotel and entered the dimly lit lobby, found a place to sit in an interior café. When they were settled, had drinks, and were all sitting opposite each other, Anna was the first to speak.

'I know what you need,' she said. 'And I could give it to you ever so easily. But then, what do I get out of it? What's my take home? I'm really going to need something from you in return. Something big.'

'We saved your life,' Reilly pointed out.

'Not that. I'm talking about something else. Something more in tune with my needs.'

'Your... needs?' Bodie didn't want to think too deeply about that one.

'Bodies,' Anna said.

HIERARCHY OF MADNESS

CHAPTER THIRTY ONE

In the dead of night, the relic hunters stalked the grounds of an old graveyard.

A drifting mist had fallen over the city, numbing the impact of the vibrant New York streets, creeping through thoroughfares and roads and boulevards. It cast its tendrils wide, encompassing Queens and Manhattan and settling even thicker over the Hudson. The effect it had was to anaesthetise everything, to bring a calm to the chaos. It also helped cover the movements of the team.

Bodie stopped close to the gates of the old graveyard. What they were about to do was crazy, especially here in the heart of Queens. But he was out of options. Cassidy came first, and the only way they were going to get Anna's line of the stanza was to play her warped and terrible game.

Jemma picked the padlock. The gates creaked as they opened. Mist drifted past Bodie's face, bringing with it the smell of smoke and home cooking. A profound silence reigned all around. Even their footfalls were muffled as they stepped into the graveyard.

Earlier, Lucie had researched some of the oldest graveyards in Queens. Anna just wanted bodies. They had to be certain they weren't dealing with anything fresh. Lucie had settled on the second oldest and jotted down the address. They had made a recce of the place, waited for pure dark, and then moved in.

In front of Bodie, the path snaked two ways, looking white in the mist. It cut between rows of gravestones, winding away. Tall, thick trees stood on both sides, their leaves hanging down, rustling in the slightest of breezes. The entire team was quiet.

In their midst, Anna beamed. Her face was softer than Bodie had seen it all day, her eyes gleaming. She fairly shook with anticipation.

Bodie hefted his rucksack over his shoulders. Inside, something clanked. He wasn't surprised. They'd been forced to purchase quite a bit of paraphernalia for this job. He walked with his eyes on a swivel, and he was grateful for the mist that concealed them.

Lucie led the way. She had a map of the graveyard printed out and led them unerringly to the right grave. This was an older, overgrown part of the graveyard where even those relatives who might tend the graves had probably passed away. To both sides sat old, pitted mausoleums and tombs with elaborate cherubs on top, with carving in their sides, with bars across their weed-choked doors. It felt as though they were creeping through another world, and not surrounded by the majesty of New York City.

Lucie arrived at the foot of the grave. She bent down to read an inscription, straightened, and then turned to the others.

'This is the one.'

Bodie unhooked his backpack and set it down. Inside, he found the foldable shovel and a few other tools. Nothing ran through his head, no thoughts of right and wrong, no sadness, no regret. It was what it was.

Cassidy came first.
Reilly, Yasmine and Heidi also had shovels. Bodie started digging first, slicing the edge of his shovel into the slightly damp, earthy ground.
I want you to dig up a body and let me see...
Anna's words.
Terrible, heart-stopping words. A disbelief and shock and disgust had fallen over Bodie the like of which he'd never felt before. Was she joking? Looking hard into her eyes, he saw she was not.
A surreal moment. Completely out of his experience.
But what could they do? Anna had the last line of the stanza. It could be the all-important line. She certainly seemed to think it was. Mixed emotions swirled through him like a twister laced with knives. A terrible, cold shock fell over his frontal lobe. When he looked around at the others, he saw the expressions on their faces and knew they felt the same.
I want you to dig up a body and let me see...
So here they were.
Bodie dug and dug. A pile of earth developed at his back. A small hole grew. He stepped into it, resumed digging. The others did the same. Lucie and Jemma stayed on watch.
Ten minutes later, there came a hiss. Jemma telling them to be quiet. Bodie paused in mid swing, looking around and breathing heavily. He could hear nothing, see very little beyond the drifting mist. He waited.
Listened.
The gloom clung to them, cold around their exposed flesh. They waited. Bodie expected to hear footsteps approaching, see a stranger in the dark, but they were in a closed-off area right now. There wouldn't be any passers-by.

Finally, Jemma shrugged, motioned at them to continue. Bodie took a moment to look up at Anna who was standing on the edge of the hole.

Her long white hair draped her shoulders, her coat twice as big as it should be. The look on her face made Bodie feel ghastly. It was full of incredible expectation, happiness. A glow came from her wide eyes. Her lips were pursed, moving slowly, as if she was singing sweet nothings to herself.

Bodie looked away. He couldn't stand it.

They worked and worked. The hole grew deeper and deeper. The mist invaded the hole and twisted its way into the freshly turned earth. Bodie lost track of time.

And then the thrust of his shovel came up short. There was a *clunk*. His wrists jarred. Yes, he'd struck something wooden.

'Shit,' he breathed.

Until that moment, it had seemed like a surreal dream. Now – right now – it was very real. He looked up at Anna.

'We can't go through with this.'

'No, carry on. *Carry on.*' She sounded ecstatic, on edge, highly excited.

'I won't dig up this body,' he said. 'This is as far as you get.'

Long, dirty strands of hair fell around the woman's face as she leaned down, looking straight at Bodie. 'Then you won't get my line. You will do this for me or I won't give it to you. And you can't force it out of me.'

Bodie closed his eyes, fought repugnance and doubt and worry and a horde of other emotions. 'You have to be...' he stopped himself.

'Crazy? Mad? Oh, yes, I know it. The urges inside me are anything but sane, and I absolutely love them.'

Anna hugged herself.

Bodie stared up at her in despair. He looked around at the faces of his team. This would haunt them for the rest of their lives.

He turned back to the hole. He could see part of the lid of the coffin now, just a wooden corner. Bodie swept at it with his hand, uncovered it. He laid his hand on it reverently.

'I'm so sorry,' he said.

Bodie continued to dig. As he did so, the others also took up their shovels to their credit and joined him. It took another five minutes to dig around the coffin and clear it off.

Bodie looked up at Lucie.

'Crowbar,' he said.

CHAPTER THIRTY TWO

'Yes, yes,' Anna whispered gleefully. 'Open it up. Let me see. *Let me see.*'

Bodie caught the crowbar that Lucie threw down to him. He moved to the side of the coffin and wedged it under the wooden surround. The coffin itself was dark oak with brass fittings and had dulled with its time underground. It looked heavy and had probably cost a lot when new.

'Wait,' Jemma said again.

They all froze, Bodie with his hand on the coffin. They listened, but heard nothing except a distant hum of traffic, the soft wind through the trees and someone shouting a long way off. A deep mist still hung over the scene.

'What is it?' Bodie hissed finally.

'That's twice I've heard some kind of shuffling noise,' Jemma said. 'I'm sure we're not alone in here.'

Bodie shivered. 'Can you see anything?'

'Not even my own hand.'

They waited, listening hard, but there were no sounds coming closer than the street that ran past the old graveyard. A truck rumbled by, its exhaust blowing, a sound that actually shattered the silence.

Anna glared at them. 'Get on with it.'

Bodie held up a hand. 'Not until Jemma gives us the okay.'

'I'm sure there's something in here with us,' she said.
'Some*thing?*' Reilly said warily.
'Could be a dog or a cat, but I definitely heard it moving.'
'So long as it's not a reanimated fucking corpse, I'm good,' Reilly said.

Bodie stuck the crowbar in the tiny gap between lid and coffin and started levering it up. It didn't move at first, and he had to apply even more pressure. Finally, there was a creak and the sound of splintered wood. The coffin lid came up a few inches.

He moved around the coffin, deciding that he would do this bit alone. Take it on himself. There was no reason for his teammates to feel this bad, to have to undertake this task. It took him a while and, all the time, Anna was practically hopping on the spot above the grave.

'Mine,' she was saying. 'All mine. All for me. This is my time.'

Bodie finished levering up the lid of the coffin. Now it just lay in place, ready to be moved. He tried with Anna one last time, just looked up at her with pity and a plea in his eyes, but she only grinned and then started capering.

'It is time,' she said.
'It doesn't have to be,' Bodie said.
'I've waited so long. So many years. They put me in prison, you know. Stopped me doing this. And now, right now, could be the best moment of my life.'

Bodie turned away and motioned at Reilly and Heidi. Together, they gripped the edges of the coffin lid. And then they heaved.

The lid came up, exposing what lay within.

Bodie let the lid fall away. He could now see inside

the coffin, saw a pitiful bundle of rags and skeletal bones in the shape of a human. There was dust in the air and the smell of something old, something long since decayed.

Anna was on her knees, staring down. Her mouth was shaped in a wide O and she was shaking.

Bodie looked up at her. 'Are you happy now?'

'I want it.'

He gaped at her, everything but the sight of her forced from his mind. *'What?'*

'I want it. Bring it to me.'

'Are you fucking kidding? I won't-'

And then Anna did something that wasn't even in Bodie's wildest imagination. His heart gave a lurch of disbelief as she flung herself from the top of the grave into the coffin.

There was a thud and the sound of old bones collapsing as she hit hard. Mushrooms of dust billowed into the air. Bodie found he was rooted to the spot, unable to move a muscle, for long seconds.

It was Reilly who broke the stasis. He leapt forward, reached in and made a grab for Anna's arms. The woman slithered free, crawling around the bottom of the coffin, slithering in the bone dust with the skeleton all around her.

Bodie grabbed the other arm, felt it wrenched free. Anna was laughing. He grabbed her again, stronger this time, and levered her up, pulled her away from the mess. When they got her upright, she turned and snarled at them.

She was like a corpse herself, white hair all grey and a face coated with bone dust. She was snarling, gnashing her teeth. Her clothes were filthy, her body wild with emotion.

Bodie yanked her towards him. Heidi joined him and grabbed at Anna's clothes. They managed to get her to the side of the coffin and then pull her out. Anna landed on the earth with a thud and looked up at them.

'Bastards,' she said.

'You desecrated that poor person's grave,' Heidi said.

'I loved it.'

Bodie collected himself, took a deep, wracking breath and then grabbed her arms. 'We did as you asked,' he said. 'We brought you to a damned corpse. Now, give us your line of the stanza.'

In her madness, in her wild and mental jubilation, Bodie thought that she might have lost it. Lost all grasp on reality. But she stared back at him now with perfect understanding.

'You did as I asked,' she said. 'I am where I want to be. But you must leave me, do you understand? You must leave me here.'

Bodie cringed. 'To do what?'

'To be with my loved one.'

'If they find you, they will put you back in jail,' Heidi said. 'Or a mental asylum.'

'If I can have one last night with my love, then that is worth it.'

Bodie held her eyes. 'The line?'

'Of course. Are you ready? *In Abaddon's Pit and the Rainbow Room.*'

Bodie took that in, memorised it. Lucie was also leaning down at that point, and repeated it out loud. They were left facing the bone dust caked woman.

'Leave me,' she said. 'I will not go any further with you.'

Bodie turned away, made his way out of the hole and

brushed himself off. He waited for the others to gather around.

'Are we leaving her?' Jemma asked.

Bodie shrugged. 'She's pretty safe here for a while. She knows the risks. And she certainly won't come with us.'

'We could knock her out,' Reilly said.

'And then we're kidnapping her. And what happens when she wakes? She'll scream in retribution. We can't take her.'

The team agreed. Bodie, out of the hole in the ground for the first time in what felt like hours, took a good look around. The surrounding gravestones stood like grey silent sentinels, embraced by rolling mists. Silence hung like a heavy blanket in the air, smothering them.

'So what's next?' Reilly asked. 'Now that we have her line.'

Lucie brightened. 'Next,' she said. 'It's research time.'

Bodie nodded, unable to shake everything that had happened since they entered the graveyard. He tried to justify it with Cassidy's peril and would move on. Eventually.

'We're not alone,' Jemma said.

Bodie looked at her. 'You mentioned that before, but this is a graveyard-'

'I heard it again. Just now. I'm sure something's moving all around us.'

For the first time, Bodie really listened. Was there a whisper in the wind? A shuffle? Some unknown presence? Was the graveyard alive with...

He shivered. His mind was playing tricks on him. After what they'd all just witnessed, he wasn't surprised. Even now, he could hear Anna crooning over her new acquaintance.

'Kill them.'

It was a whisper, but it was loud in the otherwise silent graveyard. Bodie felt a rush of fear, a wash of shock. He didn't know which way to turn.

Then came the gunshot.

The bullet flew past his head, narrowly missing. It shattered against one of the gravestones behind him. Everyone dived for the ground.

Another gunshot rang out.

CHAPTER THIRTY THREE

Bodie crawled towards the nearest gravestone. As he did so, he saw three men rise to their feet not far away. One was Raffaele, the killer holding the requisite fillet knife in his hand. The other two were more goons, and both toted handguns.

Raffaele yelled at them. 'You're too noisy. This is the fucking middle of New York. You'll have the cops all over us, idiots.'

Clearly, old Raffaele was having some leadership issues. Bodie scrambled behind a gravestone, but there were no more shots.

Heidi was to his right, Reilly to his left, both hunkered down. After a moment, they both shot to their feet.

A man dived at each of them, smashing into them around the waist and crashing to the ground. Bodie faced the grinning Raffaele.

'We meet again,' he whispered.

'You brought some proper idiots this time. Was the goon pool almost empty?'

Rafaele appeared to accept that with a shrug in the affirmative. He raised the fillet knife. 'Ready to die?'

'You people don't have much imagination, do you?'

Bodie struck first, lunging around the gravestone and hitting out at Raffaele. Fighting a man with a knife was extremely dangerous, and he wanted Raffaele at as much a disadvantage as possible.

Heidi fought one of the other men, a bruiser with a straggly beard and eyebrows you could almost grab. Her fists sank into his substantial belly, making him grunt. He was a swiper, swinging his fists in great arcs, but she was fast and avoided them. Finally, he came at her with a great bear hug. Heidi slipped around another gravestone to stay out of his reach.

Reilly kicked his man in the knee, saw him collapse to the ground. He kicked out again, trying to smash the man across the jaw and knock him out, but the guy rolled away. Reilly scrambled after him, noting how roughly he fought. This guy was just a street thug, nothing more. Which was probably why he favoured the gun.

Lucie had found a thick branch from somewhere and was circling around Raffaele, waiting for a chance to strike. Jemma crouched, ready to pounce. Yasmine joined Heidi, the two of them standing up to the huge, overweight man.

The mist circled them, writhed around them. It cast an ethereal, unreal quality over the fight. Their blows, the thumps and whacks, were all muted, dulled by the atmosphere. Even so, Bodie could still hear Anna humming in the background.

The fillet knife flashed forward. Bodie let it slip past his ribs, caught the wrist and held on. Raffaele's stepped in and tried to headbutt him. He turned his head to the side, but still felt the blow. At that moment, Lucie ran in from the back and swiped her branch at the back of Raffaele's head.

The branch snapped on impact, showering the men with splinters. Raffaele shuddered, staggered, almost fell into Bodie's arms. Bodie stepped aside and let him fall.

But Raffaele was tougher than that. He rallied fast, swinging around and thrusting with the fillet knife, forcing Bodie to keep his distance.

Heidi and Yasmine came at their huge opponent from different sides. They hit hard and fast, digging stiffened fingers and fists into the man's vulnerable areas, making him groan and stagger. When this guy went down, he wouldn't be getting back up.

Heidi found a branch on the ground, swung it. The guy couldn't get out of the way fast enough. It struck him full in the face, broke his nose. The branch was still intact. Heidi swung it again. This time, the man raised an arm, blocked the blow. The branch shattered against his thick arm.

Yasmine kicked at his knee and thigh, trying to topple him. She had found a small rock and now threw it hard. The rock connected solidly with the guy's left temple, drawing blood and making him blink. He wobbled and then collapsed to his knees. Still wary, both Heidi and Yasmine circled like predators, seeking softer areas.

Reilly waited for his opponent to make a move, confident he could counter it. The knowledge was in the man's eyes, too. He knew Reilly could take him. Reilly saw the man's hands creeping towards his gun.

He acted fast, ran in. He leapt, kneed the guy in the chest, came down with an elbow to the head. The man collapsed to his knees, the perfect height for a knee to the face. Reilly complied, sent the man toppling backwards, now out cold. He knelt over him for a moment just to make sure and then rose.

Took in the scene.

Heidi's and Yasmine's opponent was in dire straits too. Even as Reilly turned to watch, the two women ran in at the same time from opposite sides. They lashed out hard, sending the man crashing to the ground, also out cold.

Now everyone turned to Raffaele.

The killer saw it all happening. Still holding his fillet knife, he backed away.

'You're not good enough,' Bodie told him.

'I will kill you all.'

'Not today, you won't. How about telling us who sent you instead?'

'I will come back for you. I heard what that old woman told you. You will not so easily get rid of me.'

Bodie watched as Raffaele turned and stalked away. They were left in the blanket of silence, surrounded by drifting fog.

Bodie cleared his throat, turned to Lucie. 'What do we think about that last clue?'

'I think, with a bit of research, it could bear fruit.'

'This is for Cassidy,' he said. 'Everything we do is for her.'

'Just get me to my laptop.'

Bodie turned, and they all started running.

CHAPTER THIRTY FOUR

Cassidy had no choice but to continue her seduction of Arthur.

The young man was becoming increasingly enamoured of her. He was helping in any way he could, lingering over meals, bringing her treats, talking about himself. They kept the conversation low, the subject matter on the house where she was being held. When Arthur visited her, there was just one other guard, a disinterested bespectacled guy who sat on a low stool and scrolled through his phone. Cassidy had viewed him from afar, calculated the distance between the cell door and the stool, figured she could just about reach him if she acted fast.

Her plan rested on Arthur.

'You want out of here,' he said flatly now. 'You want me to help you.'

She sat on the edge of her camp bed. He stood just a few feet away, eyeing her. 'Your boss is a killer,' she whispered. 'He has no intention of releasing me.'

'I overhear them talking,' he said softly. 'They are looking forward to ending your life.'

'That's actually a nice way of putting it. I know what's coming.'

'I don't want that to happen.'

Cassidy held a hand out. Arthur took it. She smiled. In her head, she studied the problem. There were at least eighteen guards in this house, but she really only had to get past one. 'What have you heard about Bodie?' she asked.

'Only that he is searching for the last clue. He has gone to find Anna LaRoy.'

'You make it sound menacing.'

'Oh, it will be. Anna is a very difficult woman.'

'You know quite a bit about LaRoy's siblings.'

Arthur shrugged. 'Guards talk.'

'I need to get out of here, Arthur, and I need to do it now.'

'Now?'

'We're getting close to the end. Once Bodie gives LaRoy that last line, it's all over.'

'All over?'

'For me.'

Arthur chewed his bottom lip. He glanced at the locked door. Clearly, he was wondering about the guard outside. Cassidy gave his hand a squeeze.

'Will you help me?'

Her eyes filled his world. She stayed soft, gentle, unassuming. She sat there calmly, but inside she was coiled, ready to strike. Arthur checked his watch.

'Guards shift change isn't for another hour,' he said. 'This is a good time to go.'

Her heart leapt. He would give her the keys. Yes, maybe she could have overpowered him anyway but there was always the chance that their struggle would have alerted the other guard who would then come running. And then they would make her captivity harder. Arthur's cooperation changed all that.

Cassidy rose to her feet. She was ready to act. There was one last question. 'Are you coming with me, or am I going alone?'

Arthur kept hold of her hand. 'I'm going with you.'

That would be harder. She would need her hand back. 'Stick with me,' she said. 'Can you fight?'

'I've done a few lessons at the boxing gym.'

Cassidy grimaced. 'Stay behind me, then. We'll see what we can do about taking the guard out quickly and quietly.'

She walked to the door of her cell, peered through the bars. The guard was where he always was, sitting on the stool, leaning back, his big black phone in his hands. He was scrolling, betraying no emotions, just lost in another world.

Cassidy looked closer. Clearly, his hands were nowhere near his weapons. The guy had a gun holstered at his side. The holster clip was on too, which would give her precious extra seconds. She looked back at Arthur.

'Once we start this, we don't stop. Don't fall behind. Watch my back. Be prepared to fight for your life.'

His eyes shone with fear. He ran a hand through his hair, leaving half of it sticking up. Arthur wasn't ready for this.

Cassidy pointed at the door. 'Unlock it,' she said.

He moved forward and did so. Cassidy pulled it open. The guard hadn't moved. She prepared herself for a rush attack.

The guard grunted. She froze. He smiled at something on his phone, kept scrolling. Cassidy stepped out of her prison cell and ran for it.

She flew across the concrete, made up the space between her and the guard in seconds. For the first milliseconds, he didn't move, just continued to stare at his phone, but then some sixth send must have alerted him.

He looked straight at her.

Alarm creased his face. His position, slumped on the stool, made it hard for him to react. Cassidy raced up to him, threw a punch at his head. The guy scrambled to throw his hands up to ward off the blow. Cassidy had her choice of places to hit. She threw punches at his midriff, drawing his arms down, and then at his exposed skull.

He lunged around on the stool, kicking out, catching her a painful blow across the shin. She bunched her muscles and put all her strength into a couple of blows, burying her fists into his ribs and then his bicep. She leaned on him, pushed him back against the wall.

He was spluttering, fighting madly. He couldn't get up. His arms flailed. Again, he caught her with a blow, this one striking her face. The guy's nails actually ripped her skin and Cassidy felt the blood flow.

She doubled her efforts, raining the punches down. The guard fell off the stool, and it got in the way. She lifted it and brought it crashing down onto him.

He flung an arm up. There was a suspicious crack like a breaking bone and then a yell. Cassidy had got lucky. The gun was on that side, so if the bone was broken, he wouldn't be reaching for anything.

She fell to her knees beside him. She grabbed his face, prepared to smash her fists into it. The guy was at a serious disadvantage. She punched again and again, breaking the nose and then the cheekbone. The guard's eyes rolled up into his head and he slumped to the floor.

Cassidy rubbed her bruised knuckles. She rolled the guy over and took his gun from his holster, checked the mag. It was an old Glock, and it was full. Fifteen rounds. Judging by the state of it, someone had fired it a lot, which made Cassidy feel less guilty about breaking bones. Not that she'd felt particularly guilty, anyway.

She turned to Arthur. 'Now for the rest of the house.'

He nodded. She looked carefully at him. His eyes were wide, slightly glazed with fear. Arthur was a long way out of his league.

'Don't worry,' she said. 'Just stick with me.'

Of course, she could dump him now. She could knock him out. But Cassidy wasn't like that. Arthur had helped her and was willing to put his life on the line for her. It might be for unsound reasons, but it was still a commitment on his part. Cassidy wouldn't try to trick him. She would stay true to herself.

The exit door was locked. Cassidy searched the guard for the key, brought it out and introduced it to the lock. She twisted it open, turned and beckoned to Arthur.

'Stay close.'

Together, they exited the prison.

CHAPTER THIRTY FIVE

Cassidy crept through the cellars, making her way up to the ground floor of the house. It was a long, dusty way, and her route led her past barrels and bottles of wine, stacks of old, rotting boxes and bookcases full of old tomes. The strip lights flickered and fizzed, some of them dead and one of them hanging downwards. The walls were dark brick and there were a few patches of damp on the far wall.

Cassidy threaded her way through the junk. There were many winding footprints in the dust that coated the floor. She followed them to their end.

A concrete staircase leading up to a thick oak door.

Cassidy started up the stairs, taking it stealthily. Arthur followed behind, saying nothing. The poor guy was probably in shock. Cassidy felt trepidation and anxiety in her own stomach as she walked. It knotted her gut with emotion. She held the gun tighter, topped the stairs, and reached out for the door.

Steadily. Slowly. Silently.

She pushed the handle down, pulled the door open... stared a man full in the face.

He was as surprised as she was. Immediately, she realised they had placed a guard at the top of the stairs. He was a big man with brawny arms, wearing a T-shirt and a shoulder holster. His face just fell, his mouth hanging open. Cassidy couldn't shoot him. The entire house would hear. She just leapt through the door and started punching.

Her fists struck him, and he flinched. He didn't fight back straight away, just hunched over and tried to cover up. She knew she needed to end this quickly. They appeared to be in some kind of kitchen, a small one, maybe some kind of special cook's kitchen. She saw a heavy pan to her right, picked it up and smashed the guy across the head with it.

He went down, but he was still struggling, still groaning. Cassidy straddled him, lifted the pan up and then brought it crashing down into his face. The heavy cast iron impacted with his frontal lobe and he went instantly still.

Two down... lots to go, she thought.

She rose, leaving the pan on the floor. She looked around. The kitchen led deeper into the house. She would have to be quicker. These guys wouldn't stay unconscious forever and she didn't want to kill them whilst they lay comatose. She couldn't bring herself to do it.

She padded through the kitchen. Arthur spent a moment staring at the downed man and then followed. He didn't look any less terrified. Cassidy paused at the exit to the kitchen, looked through the door.

It led to a much larger kitchen, this one lined with shelves and sinks and ovens. Cassidy threaded her way down the main aisle. At the far door, she stopped again, peering through. She saw a dining room now, complete with a vast table and at least ten chairs. A chandelier hung over everything.

'It's clear,' she whispered. 'Hurry.'

They ran from the kitchen, across the dining room, to the far door. The house was silent and still. Cassidy could hear nothing, no sounds of movement, no talking, not even a cough. She wasn't sure if that was because of the size of the house or that everyone had left for the day.

No such luck.

The next room was a library, and there was a man standing in it.

The walls were lined by glass-fronted bookcases, the central area taken up by a table where, presumably, you could read your selection. There was a Tiffany lamp on the table and a plush chair beside it. Cassidy saw this guy was also armed. He had a shoulder holster and a knife at his side.

She tiptoed into the room, approached him from behind. He didn't turn. Cassidy reached up, looped an arm around his neck, and put him in a choke hold. She put all her strength into it, holding on as tightly as she could. The man brought his arms up and tried to wrench her away, but couldn't do it. Still standing, he kicked back at her shins, barking them painfully, but Cassidy ignored the shooting pains. He tried to buck her over his shoulders. Cassidy planted her feet and held on, matching his strength, staying put.

Eventually, his movements started to weaken, to cease.

He sank to his knees. She went with him, still employing the choke hold. Minutes passed. She let him slither to the floor.

She rose. Left him lying there. She passed through the library and paused at the next door.

'You are incredible,' Arthur said.

'Tell me about this house. What comes next?'

'We're in the library, so there's a living room next and then another, an even bigger one. From there, we can go down the corridor to the front door.'

'I doubt we'll be leaving through the front door. Does the living room look out onto the grounds?'

Arthur nodded.

'Then we'll exit that way. Try to find a car.'

'Won't that alert them?'

Cassidy had considered every possibility. 'I don't see another way. From the way LaRoy talked, I guessed we were on his estate, in the middle of nowhere. We could hide, yeah, but where could we go? The only way to *get away* is by car.'

'I could help with that.'

She raised an eyebrow at him. 'You mean bring it to the front door?'

'Sure. Then you jump in and we drive.'

She considered revising her plan. Would it be better to have Arthur deliver the car to the front door or steal it clandestinely? Both ways posed a hundred problems. Neither way was perfect. Should she stick to her old plan?

'I can do it,' Arthur said.

She believed him. That wasn't the issue. The issue was the placement of the guards, and she couldn't tell that without a bit of reconnoitring. Cassidy made a decision. She stole away quietly, beckoning Arthur to follow. She slipped silently through the next living room, staying low, and then entered the larger one. It was huge, full of couches and tables, desks and bureaus and sideboards littered with ornaments. In the large living room, she went to every window, tried to pin down the positions of the guards outside. She saw three walking the grounds. None of them appeared to be armed, but she knew, in reality, they would have the now ubiquitous shoulder holsters and a Glock at the ready. She finished with the windows and then took a long look down the wide corridor that led to the front of the house.

One guard stood there. He looked as if he was smoking.

'You can easily grab a car?'

'Yeah, I'll just tell them that Manny requested it.'

'And do we have any idea where Manny might be?'

Arthur checked his watch. 'It's 11 a.m. He'll be upstairs pounding at the treadmill. Manny likes to get his exercises done in the morning.'

Cassidy thought that was a stroke of luck. With the great leader out of the way, the guards might be a bit more complacent. Then she remembered LaRoy had a second-in-command called Friday. Getting away wouldn't be easy.

She'd need all the help she could get.

Well, she had three Glocks now, and she would use them if they forced her to. She watched the front door, saw the guard flick his cigarette butt away and move off. For now, they were clear.

'We'll do it your way,' she said. 'Fetch the car. I'll see you pull up through the glass.'

'It will probably be a red Dodge.'

Cassidy nodded. Arthur pushed past her, walked the length of the corridor, and approached the front door. He took one last look back, waving a hand. Cassidy cringed a little, wondering if he'd give the game away, but there was nobody around to see him.

Her heart raced as she counted off the seconds. Arthur disappeared, leaving her alone in the hallway. There were rooms leading off, and she went to check each of them, but they were all empty. LaRoy liked to keep most of his guards out of the house, it seemed.

Time passed. She grew nervous. What if Arthur

couldn't get the car, or had blabbed? Should she be looking at a contingency plan? Then, just as she was planning different scenarios in her head, there was a flash of red outside the front door.

Arthur had pulled up.

She ran down the hallway, reached the front door, and yanked it open. Fresh air hit her face and her lungs for the first time in days. She breathed hard. There were three steps leading down to the driveway and Cassidy took them now, running for the car. Arthur was in the driver's seat, beckoning her frantically.

'Hey!'

She had been expecting it. There were entirely too many guards around to make it out of here scot free, especially in a car.

She whirled. A guard had been standing idly at the corner of the house, watching Arthur. Now, when he saw Cassidy, he could see that something was wrong.

Cassidy didn't slow. She ran to the car, snatched open the door and dived in. 'Go!' she yelled.

Arthur rammed his foot down. The car roared, not in gear. The guard was now running at them and shouting into his radio. This could get bad. She yelled again, ducked down in the passenger seat as she saw the guard produce a gun.

In her haste, she'd forgotten that she was also armed.

She didn't want to start the gunfire. Maybe the guard wouldn't shoot. Arthur found the right gear and put his foot down again. The car spurted forward, tyres crunching in the gravel driveway.

The guard ran at them, aiming his weapon. Cassidy decided she needed to give him something to think about and pointed her own out the window. That brought him up short, made him dive to his left and roll. The car sped past.

Straight towards freedom.

For one second, Cassidy allowed herself to believe she was free. The open driveway beckoned and then the road. Arthur had hold of the wheel and was confidently speeding up. It was only seconds later when she realised the guard's radio call had performed some kind of purpose.

There was the roaring sound of engines. And then, in the rearview, she saw two cars chasing them, both black, both barrelling in their wake. She cursed. Why couldn't everything have just gone smoothly?

But there was no chance. The estate was just too well guarded. The following cars closed in as Arthur grew nervous at the wheel, easing off the gas slightly.

'No, speed up!' she yelled. 'They'll kill us if they catch us.'

Or rather, she thought. They'd kill *him*. But she didn't say it out loud.

The three cars sped down LaRoy's winding driveway, nose to tail. Cassidy turned so that she could look around. The car's movements jolted her from side to side, the landscape rushing by in a blur. The thing bounced and slid and shook her. She tried to hang on, turned the other way, and leaned her head out of the window.

There was a gunshot. Presumably they were aiming at the tyres. Cassidy turned again, saw the end of the driveway coming up, and had an idea.

Quickly, she brought out the Glock, aimed at the following car's tyres, and loosed off a shot. In the bouncing chaos, it missed, flew wide. She aimed again.

'We're smashing through the gates!' Arthur suddenly yelled.

Quickly, Cassidy drew her head back into the car. Just in time. There was a sudden judder, a roar, and a crash. The car smashed through the black gate. The top of the gate came down hard, smashing the windscreen, sending glass shards tumbling across Cassidy's lap. But mostly, the safety glass held.

The car skidded as it sped through the gate, but then the tyres gripped on the good asphalt road. They raced left. Arthur seemed to know where he was going.

Cassidy saw no reason not to continue her plan. The smoother road would help both her and their pursuers.

She thrust her head out of the window first, sighted the gun. Her first bullet went wide, so did her second. Then something else occurred to her. There was a much larger target inside the car. She turned her attention to the driver.

Her first bullet shattered the windscreen and struck the driver in the chest. All of a sudden, the following car started swerving and swaying from side to side. It veered to the left, swung around. The following car ploughed into it with an enormous smash of twisting metal.

Both cars were out of commission.

Cassidy was free.

She turned to Arthur. 'Get us somewhere safe. Do you have a phone?'

He pulled a face. 'Nothing, I'm afraid.'

'Never mind. We'll think of something. Just drive.'

She could barely believe it, but she had pulled off the impossible.

CHAPTER THIRTY SIX

Much earlier, the relic hunters sat in a New York city hotel, the same place they'd been sitting for most of the night. They had rented rooms because they had to, but nobody headed up to them. The lobby was the only place to be.

Lucie pulled out her laptop and did the research. Bodie never had any doubt in her. He just knew she would come through.

They sat, and they drank coffee and water and bought snacks from a nearby vending machine. Sometimes, during the night, the only sound was the tapping of Lucie's fingers. They sat back patiently, and they waited. It was a hard few hours, hoping that Lucie could get to the bottom of the mystery using one single line.

In Abaddon's Pit and the Rainbow Room.

Lucie never gave them any idea of her progress. She was totally focused. She used a notepad and her phone, taking notes from the computer. It was hours before she finally nodded to herself in satisfaction and sat back.

'I think I have something,' she said.

Everyone sat forward. Bodie, stomach churning with thoughts of Cassidy, blinked and stared at her. 'Really?' it was a hope against hope.

'Abaddon's Pit is the name of an old mine located

close to the Californian town of Jamestown. Settled around 1853, European miners arrived at the incredible diggings and started settling the town. It became one of the richest in the country with a population thousands strong. It was also one of the earliest towns to have running water,' she looked up. 'I'm just establishing its precedence.'

Bodie nodded. 'Go on.'

'As the years passed, Abaddon's hydraulic mines were merged into one whole, the Silver Spring mine, but it retained its identity because of the incredible riches it produced. It matches the rest of the lines of stanza too. Presidents and generals visited it, sipping their champagne as they were shown around. Abaddon's Pit was famous because of its diamonds, its gold, its richest gemstones. And over eighteen millions dollars' worth of gold was produced over the years. But, due to changing laws related to hydraulic mining, the local mining industry suffered setback after setback. The mines were closed and the town almost abandoned. These days, of course, it is a ghost town.'

Bodie felt elation. 'And what of this so-called rainbow room?'

'Okay, so the rainbow room is a cave inside the mine where some of the richest deposits were found. You can imagine emeralds, jade and rubies and diamonds, mined in abundance down there. You can imagine how it got its name.'

'These old mines are warrens,' Jemma said. 'You could lose yourself easily down there.'

Bodie was more conscious of the passing time and of the fact that Cassidy didn't have long. 'We're gonna have to fly to California, find this mine and get the gemstones before LaRoy knows we have the last line,' he said. 'And we have to beat Raffaele to it. Time is of the essence.'

They packed up quickly. Lucie remained on her laptop, finding and booking flights. They had little luggage with them, and it was all resting at their feet. When Lucie was done, she told them they had two hours to get to the airport.

There was no time to slow down, no rest. They were on their feet, pushing through the swing doors and calling a cab in minutes. The ride to the airport was intense. They sat in tension, in silence, worrying that LaRoy might call them for the last line of the stanza at any minute. A pall of worry hung over them, thick and curdled.

Bodie could hardly stand it. He couldn't remember ever feeling this way before. Not this intense. His worry was a living, breathing thing that curdled his insides and made his head ache. LaRoy had no idea they had found Anna yet, let alone taken her to a graveyard for the night. And Raffaele certainly wouldn't tell him. That bastard would be performing his own research.

The cab dropped them off. They passed through customs and were then forced to wait even longer for their departure time. By the time they boarded, Bodie was pacing the polished floors of the airport, trying to keep it together. They were alone in this, couldn't call anyone, couldn't get help, because they couldn't risk Cassidy's life. And the only way they could gain the leverage to do that was to locate those gemstones first.

The plane took off on its long flight. Bodie and the others tried to sleep, but got a little rest. They stayed fuelled, eating and drinking, ready to leap into action the moment they got off the plane. It touched down in California at 1 p.m., west coast time. Bodie breathed a tremendous sigh of relief when the tyres squealed across the runway, then brooded as the plane taxied towards the terminal.

Soon, they were out and through customs and walking through the balmy, warm air of a Californian day. The sun was bright, the breeze gentle and warm. There were palm trees at the airport, wafting in the winds.

Bodie saw none of it. They rented a car, punched in the ghost town's details on the sat nav and set off. Soon, Lucie was using her phone to direct them to a store that would provide them with items such as shovels, crowbars, flashlights, food and water — other items that they packed into newly purchased rucksacks. Lucie even remembered the suncream. After that, they were back in the car, ploughing through the traffic to their destination.

Hours passed. They left L.A. behind with its sweeping, hectic roads and headed out into the desert along a two-lane highway. Bodie monitored his phone as they drove, but there was still no contact from LaRoy.

Thankful, he sat back. Heidi was at the wheel, guiding them along roads that led through dusty hills and long stretches of desert. The land was brown and parched, straggly trees standing out in the middle of nowhere. The traffic was sparse, just the odd car or eighteen wheeler that blasted past them in the opposite direction.

The day marched on. The middle of the afternoon passed, and they were still driving, stopping for fuel, eating and drinking on the go. They didn't say much, just quizzed Lucie about the position of the rainbow room and the relation of Abaddon's Pit to the old ghost town. There wasn't a lot more to say.

Finally, Heidi took them down a narrow winding track that was actually posted with a 'ghost town' sign. This was where they needed to be. She followed the road for ten minutes and then they saw something new opening out up ahead.

It was the town itself. There was a wide, dusty main street with buildings running along both sides. The buildings were bleached by the sun, their facades pitted by the extremes of California's weather. A sense of solitariness hung over the town but, as Heidi pulled up, there was also the odd, unaccountable sense of being watched. Probably because of the low mountains and hills that ran all around in the hazy distance.

'Where to?' Heidi asked.

'Keep going,' Lucie said. 'You can see the old structures up ahead.'

Bodie breathed deeply as Heidi pulled up. The car could go no further due to the state of the road. Without wasting time, they climbed out into the blistering heat and pulled on their rucksacks. Bodie was already sweating. He studied the way ahead, saw the shapes of the old mine, the buildings, the century old cranes, holes cut into the rock.

They started walking, leaving the car locked behind them. Their boots trod the dusty ground, raising little mushroom clouds in their wake. They were a team, united for a single cause, ploughing forward as fast as they could. Bodie again wiped the dripping sweat from his forehead.

They passed building after building, the blank windows staring at them like soulless eyes. It was incredibly quiet – all these structures, all once full of human beings and the noise they make, now standing empty. It all added to the sense of being watched.

To the right, a space opened out. It was now just a dusty yard, but had once been a tiny park. An old swing set stood there, rusted, creaking slightly and eternally, propelled by the breeze. A broken bike lay next to it, covered in filth and weeds.

Bodie kept going. They left the town behind and approached the outskirts of the mine. There was a fairly recent sign in front that read: DANGER. Bodie noticed, with trepidation, that it had been shot several times. They passed several more warning signs as they made their way up the slope that led to the mine.

Lucie used her phone as they went, calling up old maps of the mine. Once, years ago, it had been retooled into a tourist attraction; the locals trying to come up with a proactive idea but, eventually, the lack of customers had caused it to shut down. Still, the old maps issued by the mine company were still online.

'Are we there yet?' Yasmine asked drily.

Bodie kept walking, kept his head down. Reilly and Heidi were monitoring their perimeter, looking out for any unwanted guests. So far, they hadn't even seen a coyote wandering the desert.

Bodie reached the foot of the slope that led to the main cave. He turned to Lucie.

'Is this it?'

Lucie squinted at the map. 'Good job I screenshotted these when I had a signal,' she said. 'I can't get anything way out here.'

Bodie waited.

'It's the main entrance to Abaddon's Pit,' Lucie said finally, comparing her map to the landscape, the rocks, the rolling hills.

'And the rainbow room?'

'It's a fair way in. Put it this way, it's a good job we brought those flashlights.'

Bodie looked at the mine, its dark entrance forbidding and disconcerting. There were old wooden supports on both sides, probably the remains of a more welcoming entrance at one time. The wood was rotting, one timber hanging away from the wall. To the left, the main paraphernalia of the mine stood in old, disused splendour.

He called the others to him.

'This is it,' he said, taking a swig of water. 'We have to get in, find the gemstones, and then get out as quickly as possible. Then we find a signal and call that bastard LaRoy.'

'We offer an exchange,' Heidi said. 'The gemstones for Cassidy.'

'That's it,' Bodie said. 'Any questions?'

There were none. They had to move fast. They knew also that Raffaele had the same information that they did and that he also might have a capable researcher. Even a half-capable one could pull up the information from the internet in a few hours.

They unhooked their rucksacks, took out torches and flashlights, fixed helmet lights to their heads. They checked on the shovels and crowbars and other items, made sure they had everything with them.

And then they started towards the mine entrance, moving fast.

CHAPTER THIRTY SEVEN

Inside the mine, it was dank and dark and fusty.

Bodie led the way, the others close to his back. He shone his flashlight ahead. Shadows leapt and escaped the light, rushing away. He smelled old things, something damp and chilly. The rock walls were smooth here, as if they been touched by thousands of hands through the years. He walked further in and then came to a large chamber which looked as if it had been hewn from the rock. Probably had. Those old miners were determined.

He saw a surprising amount of junk on the ground. Old helmets. A wrinkled shirt. Gloves that may or may not be hundreds of years old. He didn't have the time to stop and look. The darkness, the state of the mines, told them they should take their time. It clearly wasn't safe. But Bodie had Cassidy on his mind.

Lucie told him which way to go. They reached two junctions almost immediately. Staying true to character, Lucie remained sensible, taking the time to leave something wedged on the ground, showing them the route when they returned despite the map in her hand. It was far better to be safe than sorry. Bodie saw narrow rock walls, smelled ancient dust. They found an old machine that would shake the gemstones from the rock, sorting them. They found a stash of old boots, rotted with age. There were several niches cut into the walls where, once, things had been stored, and they found several items here, too. It was a strange, silent journey, punctuated by the sound of their boots on the rocky floor of the cave.

As he followed a narrow passage, Bodie saw, to the right, a shiny deposit. It caught his eye, flashing in the lights of the torches. Was it a gemstone after all this time? He slowed slightly to study it as he passed, rubbed the rock. It was jagged and hard; the deposit shining with a slightly greenish hue. Bodie experienced a moment of awe. This was how the old miners must have felt when they found something precious.

He walked on. Lucie paused to take a photo of the deposit. The rest walked straight by, focused. They came through another cavern, this one much smaller but packed with old junk. Hats. Coats. Tools. There were a few more machines, but Bodie couldn't even begin to guess their purpose. In the far corner, there were piles of old bones, another mystery. He continued out of the chamber and along another passage.

Lucie kept on reading out the directions. It felt like a long sluggish slog, but that was because they were forced to slow down, to keep an eye on their environs. Once, Bodie squeezed through a narrow constriction of rolling walls to find an empty space to his right. No matter how he angled his torch or shined it downwards, he found an absolute absence of, well... anything. It might as well have been a bottomless pit.

They slowed down after that.

Bodie kept going doggedly. He wouldn't let up. He passed tiny glitters of gold set into stone. Something that glowed blue. He stumbled over a set of tools, kicked them aside, the sudden noise setting all their hearts beating fast.

Ahead, and perfectly located with Lucie's map, a tiny stream crossed their path. It was a great position finder. Lucie let out a deep sigh of relief. She was just happy she'd led them down the right track. Bodie hadn't doubted her, and had put his life in her hands. His eyes were tired of squinting, and staring into the bright light of the torch reflected off shiny rock. His legs ached. His stomach continued to roil.

'It's just ahead,' Lucie said softly.

So softly, in fact, Bodie barely heard her. He slowed, paused, turned.

'What? Where?'

'Should be just in front of us.'

Bodie shone the flashlight ahead. The tunnel got a little higher here, and it was shaped into an archway like a grand entrance. Maybe the old miners had made something special of the so-called rainbow room. Maybe, because they spent so much time down here, they had turned it into a spectacle.

The archway currently led toward blackness. Bodie started walking forward.

'Be prepared for anything,' he said.

CHAPTER THIRTY EIGHT

Bodie stalked forward.

The flashlight gradually revealed the rainbow room in all its glory. It was a wide, lofty chamber, curved at the top. It hung with stalactites, long dangerous looking prongs. The sides were rocky and jagged, the floor relatively smooth. Certain areas had been shored up with old timbers, and there were dozens of niches cut into the old walls. The smell inside was quite fresh, as if it had some kind of ventilation, maybe an old, hidden shaft that led outside.

Bodie knew he stood inside one of the most spectacular mines in history, in the rainbow room. He took a single moment to breathe deeply and then started looking around. Certain things caught his attention, but not the things he wanted to see.

There were the creaking timbers holding up part of the room. Even from here, they looked frail but, luckily; it wasn't the primary structure and just confined to two of the sides. There were undulations of rock running around the walls, and in these undulations, colours glimmered. He saw all the colours of the rainbow in the lights of the torches as his colleagues squeezed in behind him and started spreading out around the room.

Flashes of green and red and blue shimmered in the lights, sparkling suddenly as each random torch touched it. There was gold too, and the clean light of things that could only be diamonds. These weren't large stones. There wasn't a fortune lying here – it was simply shards and cuttings and remnants that the old miners hadn't been able to take away, shavings of splendour, all catching the light.

But Bodie could definitely see where the room got its name.

Maybe the old miners had left the fragments on purpose. Maybe it was just a shiny old remnant of a bygone age. Whatever it was, it was stunning.

Lucie rushed forward, trying to take it all in. Her eyes were everywhere, her head twisting from side to side. She let out a cry of delight. The others spread out around Bodie, equally impressed with the rainbow room.

'Incredible,' Lucie breathed.

Bodie tried to stay focused. It was easy to get lost in the shimmering colours, in the natural deposits, the greens and reds and blues. But they couldn't spare the time. He took a good look around. Rock surrounded them. Where would LaRoy's father have deposited the gemstones?

After everything they'd been through, he was hoping for a break. At first, he didn't get it. He looked high and low, inspecting all the niches first. One by one, the others got over their initial wonder and started helping. The team spread out around the room and began searching in earnest.

And then, from the far corner of the room, Lucie let out a yell. There were more niches running along the back and several of those niches were only half depth.

'It has to be this,' she said. 'Something's hidden behind this fake layer. It's like hardpan. Hardened clay.

A fake wall. I think you will find one of these niches will hold what we're looking for.'

Bodie came froward and studied the niches. They looked genuine, but then that was the whole point. He brought out the crowbar and started smashing into the rock. The hardpan flaked away and then cracked and crumbled. When the false wall fell away, Bodie peered down to get a good look inside the niche.

'Nothing,' he said, on his hands and knees.

'Keep trying,' Lucie urged him.

Bodie attacked the next niche and then the next. He got no joy. His limbs and joints ached with the effort of wielding the crowbar. Reilly saw the struggle and took over.

They broke open twelve niches. LaRoy's father, if he'd done all this, must have had a great time leaving the false niches for his siblings to find. Bodie imagined him cackling to himself as he made false niche after false niche, happy in his madness. Everything he did was to the detriment of his sons and daughters.

With the thirteenth niche, they struck lucky.

The hardpan cracked, fell away. Reilly peered inside. Bodie saw his entire frame stiffen and knew there was something in the hole.

'I think this is it,' Reilly said.

The team crowded forward. Jemma reached in and tried to grab something, but pulled away.

'Too heavy,' she said.

They laid down, reached out, and took hold of something. Bodie got his first good look into the niche. Inside, there was a large chest, black in colour, with a silver lock. It measured about two feet in length and about one and a half in height. Together, they dragged it out of the niche. The chest came with a heavy scraping noise.

Finally, it sat at their feet. Bodie knelt down before it, studied the lock. He didn't stand on ceremony, just employed the crowbar in the best way possible. On another day, at another time, when time hadn't been running so hard against them, a terrible competitor, he'd have taken more time. But not today.

The lock snapped. Heidi reached out and lifted the lid. Bodie took a deep breath, hoping against hope that they'd found the right thing.

The chest's lid came up, treating them to an incredible sight. The chest was full to the brim with sparkling gemstones, all piled and packed and stacked against each other. There were heaps of rubies, masses of emeralds, mounds of jade. There were shiny, glittering diamonds and much more. Other stones, not so recognisable but equally impressive. Everything shimmered in the light, throwing off myriad rainbows.

Bodie sat back. Lucie reached out, dug her hands into the shiny heaps and lifted two handfuls, let them run through her fingers back into the chest. Heidi copied her. The team didn't speak for entire minutes.

Finally, Bodie came back to the job at hand. They didn't have any time to waste. He rose quickly to his feet.

'Time to get the hell out of here,' he said.

'Oh, I wouldn't move quite so fast if I were you,' a voice rang out behind them.

Bodie turned, off balance. From the shadows at the entrance to the cavern, a shape emerged. Almost immediately, Bodie knew it was the killer, Raffaele.

'You followed us?' he asked.

Raffaele moved slowly in the semi-dark, a shadow snaking through the gloom. He appeared to be alone.

'I heard the same information as you,' he said.

'Abaddon's Pit. Rainbow Room. I can put in the research too.'

'Where's your goons?' Heidi asked, seeking her own information.

Raffaele slunk forward a little more. 'It appears I can rely on no one but myself,' he said. 'So here I am.'

Bodie started to move, wondering at Raffaele's emboldened actions. They were one against six, after all. Then he saw the gun in Raffaele's hand.

'Don't move,' the killer said.

'We can make a deal,' Heidi said.

'A deal? Why would I want to make a deal? I have the gun.'

'We have the chest,' Yasmine pointed out.

'Not for long,' Raffaele took another step forward.

Bodie could see him better in the light now. The curly blonde hair, the feline face stretched in a rictus of hatred. There was no doubt in his mind that Raffaele intended to kill them and leave their bodies in the endless dark. 'Spread out,' he murmured to the team.

They did, making harder targets. Bodie stayed with the chest. He switched his helmet light off and the others did the same. Now, all that illuminated the cavern were their handheld flashlights.

They had to take a chance; he knew. Raffaele would never let them live. But he could only come up with one plan of action, and it was a risky one.

But not as risky as getting shot to death.

In the half-dark, he communicated his plan to Jemma, told her to pass it on. Raffaele was staring at the open box.

'So that's what it's all about,' he breathed. 'So much wealth.'

'Your boss wants it all for himself,' Bodie said. 'And will get our friend killed.'

'Cassidy Coleman? She's dead already.'

Bodie felt a rush of anxiety and fear. He didn't believe it. 'No way would LaRoy risk that,' he said. 'Even he isn't that insane.'

Raffaele shrugged. 'It does not matter. I just want the box.'

'And then you're going to kill us?'

'Of course not. I'll leave you here, wounded, to die slowly.'

Raffaele waved the gun up and down. 'Now,' he said. 'Move away.'

Bodie knew he was preparing to shoot them. He just wanted them clear of the box. It was now or never. With a surreptitious look at his friends, he took a deep breath, nodded, and then threw his flashlight straight at Raffaele.

The others did the same.

There was instant darkness, flashing light, beams rolling through the air, tumbling. There was the clatter of plastic hitting flesh. A gunshot.

The team leapt forward, straight at Raffaele.

Flashlights had struck the man and fallen away, and were now shining randomly around the room, catching the rainbow light. Bodie and the others ran through this flickering iridescence like shadows flitting through a kaleidoscope, racing for their quarry. Reilly was the first to hit, striking the man hard. The gun went off, a bullet flashing over Reilly's head to hit the rocky roof.

Raffaele went down. The others landed on him. Reilly fought for the gun. Bodie ran in fast, trod on one of Raffaele's flailing hands. They were six on one, but the killer wasn't done yet.

He dropped the gun, heaved his body up from the ground. He rolled, escaped their grips, and then there was the flash of the fillet knife.

Bodie, elated, reached down to pick up the gun, grabbed it off the ground. He raised it and aimed it at Raffaele.

But the killer had the magazine in his left hand, and he was grinning.

Fuck, Bodie thought.

Raffaele came in with the knife, jabbing carefully. Lucie dived out of the way and rolled. Yasmine blocked but caught an edge to the wrist, gasped. Raffaele didn't stop, just slashed away at the team as he cut his way through them. It was a terrible onslaught, leaving blood in its wake. Bodie saw a killer wielding a knife at the top of his game.

He rolled away, the rock of the cave floor hard on his back. He came up. Raffaele was there. Bodie pretended to lash out, to overreach. Raffaele dodged the blow and then came in fast and hard with the knife.

But Bodie was ready for him.

He jumped up and kicked out with both feet, landed hard on his tailbone. But it was worth it. Raffaele ran straight into the kicking feet, staggered, and went flying to the side. He still had hold of the knife, but couldn't help himself from getting propelled into the timbers that shored up part of the left-hand wall.

He crashed into the timbers, throwing up a mushroom cloud of dust. The wood snapped and split along its length. Raffaele went down. Above him, part of the rock wall groaned.

Raffaele was on his back, looking up.

He screamed when the rock wall came down, a tumble of large stones and shale and boulders. He didn't scream again. The rocky stream surged down on him, buried him. Bodie saw one rock crack his skull open. The fillet knife fell away as the rock continued to fall.

Bodie acted fast. With Reilly, he grabbed the chest and started to run. They scooped up their flashlights, used the four that weren't broken, and started running back the way they'd come. They fled along tunnel after tunnel, following the markers; Lucie out in front. Bodie panted heavily, his face coated with grime, his forehead dripping with sweat. The chest between him and Reilly weighed heavily.

At last, they saw the light ahead. Bodie, elated, took a deep breath and smiled. The light meant they were almost free, almost free to negotiate Cassidy's safe release. The chest represented all the leverage they would need.

Without slowing down, the team exited the mine at speed.

Bodie was already running through the next phone call in his head. He would call LaRoy up, tell him he'd already found the chest, and start negotiations. LaRoy would have no choice but to hand over Cassidy if he wanted the chest at all.

And Bodie was willing to give it to him for Cassidy's safe return.

Sunlight slammed into his eyes, hurting them.

When he stopped blinking, he saw a terrible sight and heard a man's voice.

'Hey,' the guy said. 'I'm Friday, LaRoy's second in command. Good to see you. I'm so glad I decided to take matters into my own hands.'

CHAPTER THIRTY NINE

Bodie squinted hard, his eyes gradually adjusting to the light.

Before him stood a well-built man holding a machine gun. This would be LaRoy's traitor then, Raffaele's contact. To the left and right of the man stood others, all armed, four in total. They were all standing confidently, some smirking, most of them eyeing the chest between Bodie and Reilly.

'Give it to me.' Friday's eyes were greedy, and he licked his lips.

'Aren't you wondering where your mate, Raffaele, is?' Bodie played for time as the team inched closer and closer to the standing men.

'Since you're here, I'm assuming he's dead. But I don't really care.'

'He's lying there injured,' Bodie lied. 'We were about to go back and get him.' Another two steps closer.

'Such a shame,' Friday said. 'For him. Now stop where you are and give me that chest.'

What happened next came naturally to Bodie, and their time working together must be paying off, because it came naturally for Reilly, too. It was a wild, instant decision. They swung the chest between them, got some momentum going, and then flung it up into the air as high as it would go.

Friday gawped, staring at it. His eyes followed the chest, as did all the other men. It was the best Bodie could have hoped for.

With the chest in the air, they attacked. They leapt at the gunmen, wrestling for their weapons. Bodie and Reilly hit first, tackling Friday and another man. Yasmine and Heidi came next, leaping in as fast as they could. Jemma and Lucie assaulted the last opponent, working together.

It was a mad tussle. The relic hunters fought for the weapons, struggling across the hard ground. They staggered, somehow managed to hang onto their opponents. It was a fraught, insane few minutes. There was yelling and grunting and point-blank screaming. Bodie had hold of Friday's weapon and was keeping it pointed at the ground, but that allowed Friday the freedom to headbutt his face, splitting his lip. Seeing his success made Friday do it again, and Bodie felt a tooth chip.

To his left, Reilly was faring better. He'd got a good grip on his opponent and broken the man's wrist. The gun was on the floor between their boots, getting kicked around in the dust. Reilly pushed his man hard, striking at the solar plexus, and sent him stumbling away.

Reached down, picked up the gun and shot him.

Bodie kicked out at Friday's left knee. His boot struck true. The man yelled and slithered away. He yanked on the gun arm, but Friday held on.

But now he had Reilly's gun pointed at his head.

'Put your gun down,' Reilly said. 'And tell your men to stop fighting.'

Friday snarled. He struck out at the gun, almost

swatted it from Reilly's hand. Bodie took the opportunity to punish the man's stomach with a crushing blow.

Friday fell to his knees. Reilly pushed his gun in the man's face.

'Stand down,' he said.

Friday struck out again, unwilling to give in. His blow sailed aimlessly by and Reilly smacked him on the head with the barrel of his gun.

'Last chance.'

To the right, Yasmine and Heidi were matched to their opponents. It was a silent death struggle, a battle of strength and muscle and cunning. Neither side wanted to give up ground, so they stood face to face, grappling for the gun. The men tried to rip their arms from the grips of the women. Beside them, Lucie had hold of her opponent's gun and was forcing it in the opposite direction. It was an almost silent, deadly struggle, the only sound the constant shuffling of feet.

The harsh sunlight beat down on them. It was dry, dusty, and hot. The only people for miles around were those battling beneath the vivid skies.

Bodie slipped and fell to his knees, still fighting Friday. Reilly had finally had enough. He had to show Friday that he wasn't bluffing. He stepped back, took aim, and fired a shot into the meat of Friday's right thigh.

The man screamed, fell to one knee. Bodie wrenched his gun from his hand, twisting it away. Instantly, he turned to the other battles.

'Stop fighting!' he shouted. 'Give up your guns or I'll shoot.'

The men glanced at him, seeing the futility of their situation. Friday, their boss, was out of the fight. Bodie and Reilly could pick any of them off at any moment. And the women they fought against weren't exactly backing down.

One by one, they gave up, throwing their guns to the ground. Bodie sidestepped as Friday, even injured, lashed out again, almost foaming at the mouth. He watched as Heidi and Yasmine scooped up the other guns and then trained them on their enemies.

The chest had landed on its side, spilling out piles of gemstones. Lucie ran to it now, refilling it and closing the lid once more.

'Stay here,' Bodie said. 'Don't try to follow us. We need this chest and will kill to keep it.'

The team took a few steps away from their enemies, creating distance and levelling the guns. The men, breathing heavily, eyed them warily. Friday groaned on the ground, giving them an evil glare.

Right then, as Bodie watched everything with an eagle-eyed stare, his phone started buzzing. The signal must have come back now that they were out of the caves. He nodded to Reilly, letting him cover Friday, and assumed the caller was LaRoy.

'Might as well get this over right away,' he said, reaching for the phone.

He didn't check the screen, just pushed the answer button.

'LaRoy,' he began. 'We have your gemstones, but-'

'It's me,' a voice interrupted him.

Bodie blinked. His heart soared. 'Cassidy?'

'Yeah, who else? I got out. I'm free.'

It felt like the weight of the world lifting off his shoulders. 'Oh, my... how... when... oh, that's fantastic news.'

The others were all watching him from the corners

of their eyes, taking vital attention away from their captives. Bodie quickly turned to them and shouted, 'Cassidy got away!'

There were smiles, cheers, the pumping of fists. The team just couldn't stop grinning. Bodie turned back to the phone.

'Are you hurt? Are you safe?'

'I'm in New York. I called the cops and spoke to a Detective Wright who's handling my case. Said he knew you from the crime scene.'

Bodie remembered Detective Wright had been the man in charge when they visited Cassidy's abduction scene. 'Yeah, he helped us early on.'

'Wright's due to interview me this morning. I'm gonna give him everything on LaRoy.'

It sounded perfect. Cassidy's testimony would bring down LaRoy; the police would visit his estate, probably find all kinds of incriminating evidence. That part was beautiful, but the genuine joy was that Cassidy was alive and free and unhurt. His heart was pounding in his chest, his mouth dry with excitement.

'Oh, Cass,' he said. 'I'm so glad to hear your voice.'

'It was touch and go there for a while. Where the hell are you guys, anyway?'

Bodie told her it was a long story and that they'd catch up soon. All the while, Friday and his men were staring at them with anger in their eyes. He didn't care. All of this had been about Cassidy. Even now, with the chest in their possession, he'd been sure LaRoy would somehow weasel it away from them and still hurt Cassidy. He couldn't get the idea out of his head; it clung like a leech, whispering to him every second.

But now... now... it was perfect.

'Back to the car,' he told the team, and then

addressed Friday and his men. 'You guys can give us a fifteen minute head start. Then you're free to do as you wish.'

A few of the men looked surprised, as though they'd been expecting a bullet. Friday still snarled at them and looked a little disappointed, either because Cassidy had escaped or because he'd already known and had been keeping the bombshell to himself.

Bodie and the others backed away from Friday and his men, got into their car and turned it on. They still pointed their guns out of the windows, trained on their enemies. Bodie sat himself down in the passenger seat, the chest sitting on his knees.

'Well,' he said. 'It looks like our money troubles are over.'

Lucie leaned forward from the back as Reilly set the air conditioning on full. 'Doesn't it belong to the LaRoy family estate?'

'I doubt it, but we can check, I guess. It's fair game as far as I'm concerned. Fair relic hunter spoils.'

'At least there should be a reward,' Yasmine said.

'Or we could sell the stash to a museum,' Heidi said. 'The Met would be fitting.'

'Either way, we're not scraping our last dollars together anymore,' Bodie said. 'I'd say that's a win-win.'

'And then we start our own company,' Bodie said. 'Together. A team. An organisation. We have the contacts.'

'But our biggest win ever is on the other end of that phone,' Heidi said, referring to Cassidy.

Bodie breathed a sigh of relief as Reilly backed out of the mine and then turned the car around. It had been a breakneck, headlong chase, a worry-fraught few days, a real tapestry of fear. He couldn't remember even feeling so scared. Now, though, everything had changed. LaRoy was about to get his comeuppance. And they had relic hunter spoils in their possession.

THE END

Thanks for reading the latest *Relic Hunter* instalment. I really hope you enjoyed it and look forward to the new direction the series will now take. The next release will be Joe Mason 4 in October, *The Babylon Plot,* and then look for a new Matt Drake in November!

If you enjoyed this book, please leave a review or a rating.

DAVID LEADBEATER

Other Books by David Leadbeater:

The Matt Drake Series
A constantly evolving, action-packed romp based in the escapist action-adventure genre:

The Bones of Odin (Matt Drake #1)
The Blood King Conspiracy (Matt Drake #2)
The Gates of Hell (Matt Drake 3)
The Tomb of the Gods (Matt Drake #4)
Brothers in Arms (Matt Drake #5)
The Swords of Babylon (Matt Drake #6)
Blood Vengeance (Matt Drake #7)
Last Man Standing (Matt Drake #8)
The Plagues of Pandora (Matt Drake #9)
The Lost Kingdom (Matt Drake #10)
The Ghost Ships of Arizona (Matt Drake #11)
The Last Bazaar (Matt Drake #12)
The Edge of Armageddon (Matt Drake #13)
The Treasures of Saint Germain (Matt Drake #14)
Inca Kings (Matt Drake #15)
The Four Corners of the Earth (Matt Drake #16)
The Seven Seals of Egypt (Matt Drake #17)
Weapons of the Gods (Matt Drake #18)
The Blood King Legacy (Matt Drake #19)
Devil's Island (Matt Drake #20)
The Fabergé Heist (Matt Drake #21)
Four Sacred Treasures (Matt Drake #22)
The Sea Rats (Matt Drake #23)

Blood King Takedown (Matt Drake #24)
Devil's Junction (Matt Drake #25)
Voodoo soldiers (Matt Drake #26)
The Carnival of Curiosities (Matt Drake #27)
Theatre of War (Matt Drake #28)
Shattered Spear (Matt Drake #29)
Ghost Squadron (Matt Drake #30)
A Cold Day in Hell (Matt Drake #31)
The Winged Dagger (Matt Drake #32)
Two Minutes to Midnight (Matt Drake #33)

The Alicia Myles Series

Aztec Gold (Alicia Myles #1)
Crusader's Gold (Alicia Myles #2)
Caribbean Gold (Alicia Myles #3)
Chasing Gold (Alicia Myles #4)
Galleon's Gold (Alicia Myles #5)
Hawaiian Gold (Alicia Myles #6)

The Torsten Dahl Thriller Series

Stand Your Ground (Dahl Thriller #1)

The Relic Hunters Series

The Relic Hunters (Relic Hunters #1)
The Atlantis Cipher (Relic Hunters #2)
The Amber Secret (Relic Hunters #3)
The Hostage Diamond (Relic Hunters #4)
The Rocks of Albion (Relic Hunters #5)

The Illuminati Sanctum (Relic Hunters #6)
The Illuminati Endgame (Relic Hunters #7)
The Atlantis Heist (Relic Hunters #8)
The City of a Thousand Ghosts (Relic Hunters #9)

The Joe Mason Series

The Vatican Secret (Joe Mason #1)
The Demon Code (Joe Mason #2)
The Midnight Conspiracy (Joe Mason #3)
The Babylon Plot (Joe Mason #4)

The Rogue Series

Rogue (Book One)

The Disavowed Series:

The Razor's Edge (Disavowed #1)
In Harm's Way (Disavowed #2)
Threat Level: Red (Disavowed #3)

The Chosen Few Series

Chosen (The Chosen Trilogy #1)
Guardians (The Chosen Trilogy #2)
Heroes (The Chosen Trilogy #3)

DAVID LEADBEATER

Short Stories
Walking with Ghosts (A short story)
A Whispering of Ghosts (A short story)

All genuine comments are very welcome at:

davidleadbeater2011@hotmail.co.uk

Twitter: @dleadbeater2011

Visit David's website for the latest news and information:
davidleadbeater.com

Printed in Great Britain
by Amazon